DO NOT OPEN UNTIL
Christmas

DO NOT OPEN UNTIL
Christmas

JEAN LITTLE

Red Deer Press

Published in Canada by Red Deer Press,
195 Allstate Parkway, Markham, Ontario L3R 4T8

Published in the United States by Red Deer Press,
311 Washington Street, Brighton, Massachusetts 02135

www.reddeerpress.com

10 9 8 7 6 5 4 3 2 1

"Without Beth" copyright © 1994 by Jean Little from
The Unexplained: A Haunted Canada Book © 2008 by Scholastic Canada Ltd.
From *What Will the Robin Do Then?* by Jean Little. Copyright © Jean Little, 1998.
Reprinted by permission of Penguin Canada Books Inc.

Red Deer Press acknowledges with thanks the Canada Council for the Arts,
and the Ontario Arts Council for their support of our publishing program.
We acknowledge the financial support of the Government of Canada
through the Canada Book Fund (CBF) for our publishing activities.

Library and Archives Canada Cataloguing in Publication
ISBN 978-0-88995-527-1. ISBN 978-0-88995-528-8
Data available on file

Publisher Cataloging-in-Publication Data (U.S.)
ISBN 978-0-88995-527-1. ISBN 978-0-88995-528-8
Data available on file

Edited for the Press by Peter Carver
Text & cover design by Tanya Montini
Cover image courtesy of Aino Anto

Printed in Canada

Contents

Dedication

This book is dedicated to Michele Landsberg,
Ken Setterington, and Shelagh Rogers—and all who have served
on the CBC Children's Book Panel—because of their contagious
delight in telling us about great books for children.

The Portable Christmas

The Penny twins were the last to leave the warm classroom. The other kids were almost out of sight when Nick pulled shut the door of the portable. He jumped the steps and headed for home.

Holly slipped on the icy second step and almost fell flat on her face in the wet snow. She waved her arms, caught her balance, made it safely to the ground, and gave the portable a baleful backward glance.

"I hate portables," she muttered. "Everything in our lives is portable now, Nick. Did you realize that?"

Her brother slowed down until she was at his side. He did not ask her what she was going on about. He knew. He also knew he had better let her get it out of her system, or she'd go on grumping and groaning all the way home.

"Ever since Mom and Dad got divorced," she said, "we've had

to pack up every other second and go somewhere else. Two weeks here, two weeks there. I hate moving every other weekend. The stuff I need is always at the other place. And Christmas is awful. Remember last year?"

Nick did remember. He grimaced but did not interrupt her.

"We had to move around all day long. Get up and open presents at Mom's. Leave those gifts behind. Get picked up and open more presents at Dad's. Leave the new stuff behind, even if it was a book or a game. Then drive to Grandpa and Grandma's and open more. Stick those in a bag to take home to Mom's. And then go all the way out to the country to see Great Grandpa and …"

"I remember," Nick broke in at last. "I was there, too. It was not the best Christmas ever. But we're stuck with it. It'll be the same this year, except for everyone making even more fuss over the Revolting Child—otherwise known as Baby Susie."

"You know what, Nick? Dad should have called her Mistletoe if he wanted her to fit in and be our true baby sister. We could call her Mistletoe." Holly's voice was high and a little shrill.

"No, we couldn't. She wasn't born on December 25," Nick said mildly. "She's only a baby. She'll probably improve."

"Don't count on it," Holly said, kicking at an inoffensive tree trunk that was near the sidewalk. "But it's not really Susie that makes everything so disgusting. It's the way we don't matter any longer. We're like parcels. They can't leave us behind, but they never

DO NOT OPEN UNTIL CHRISTMAS

bother to open us and see what's inside."

They trudged on in silence for a couple of blocks. Then Holly burst into speech once again.

"We shouldn't have been born on Christmas," she fumed. "Why did we rush like that? We could have been born in February if we'd just hung on."

Nick laughed.

"With our luck, it would have been February 14, and Mom would have named us Cupid and Valentina," he snorted.

Holly had to laugh, too. But there was misery just under the laughter. Their parents' divorce had made everything harder, but their Christmassy names had been a burden from the day their Grade 1 teacher, Miss Brigson, had gushed about them in front of the whole class.

A far-off voice chanted:

"Prickle and Nickel

Are sour as a pickle."

The twins did not even look around. They were used to being called names. They had had five Christmas seasons of it by now.

"If only Miss Brigson hadn't noticed," Holly said again.

"Yeah," Nick said.

Holly almost always talked for both of them. It was one of the things that drove their stepmother crazy.

"Why, your birthday is December 25," Miss Brigson had said in a voice that carried to every corner of the classroom. "Your mother must have been thrilled to have twins for Christmas. A double present. I should have noticed your names. Holly Carol and Nicholas Noel. How sweet!"

They had not looked at each other, but their hearts had plummeted into their shoes. All they could do was hope that the kids would have forgotten before December arrived. They hadn't.

Then, to top it off, Miss Brigson had made things worse by loving the carols that Holly and Nick had grown to loathe.

"The holly bears a prickle," she had taught the class, "as sharp as any thorn …"

The other kids grinned even as they sang. The twins had been Prickle and Nickel from that day on. What did all of it matter? Christmas was coming and they had to get through it. Another portable Christmas.

"We should go on strike or something," Nick said idly.

And right then, Holly had her magnificent idea. She opened her mouth to blurt it out, and then made herself wait until she thought it through. She had to work out the details. If she were to get Nick to go along with her, she had to think of every possible snag.

By Christmas Eve, they had perfected each detail of the plan. Nick had been persuaded without too much trouble. Holly went to bed, feeling sick to her stomach with excitement. If only Nick didn't chicken out at the last minute and refuse to come!

 4

She had her little alarm clock under her pillow, but she did not need it to ring. She felt as though she had not slept at all and, at four o'clock, she eased out of bed and crept into Nick's room. To her astonishment, he was sleeping soundly. She put her hand over his mouth to rouse him. His eyes flew open at once.

"Come on," she breathed.

He slid out of bed. He was already dressed. They had put their clothes back on the minute Mom had left their rooms the night before. Holly knelt to get the gym bag out from under his bed. They tiptoed downstairs and made for the front door.

Then Nick remembered the note.

Holly went back and put it on the mantel above the fake fireplace. Mom would spot it eventually. They had put it in a small, plain envelope so it might not catch her eye for a while. That suited the twins. The scariest part was unlocking the front door and shutting it again, without making a betraying click.

"This is the first time in my life that I've been glad we don't have a dog," Nick whispered.

They tiptoed down the drive past the other townhouses and then, feeling safe at last, they ran. The snow had melted days ago. It was going to be what people called "a green Christmas," although the twins saw nothing green about it. All the visible grass was brown and dead looking. Who cared? They walked to the bus stop and waited.

"Maybe it won't be running on Christmas," Nick said.

"It will," Holly said. "I checked. We're just early."

Finally, before it was fully light, the bus pulled up. The children climbed on and said, "Merry Christmas," to the driver.

"Where are you two bound? Do your parents know you're out?" he asked.

"Of course they do. They arranged for us to go to our grandfather's," Holly said, gazing at him with her innocent eyes. Nick, who was a transparent liar, kept his head down and his mouth shut.

They took the subway after that, and then the Greyhound bus from the terminal. Once they were seated near the back and nobody seemed to be noticing them, Holly slumped down in relief and fell asleep. Nick was the one who watched, afraid they would fail to get off in Guelph. It seemed to take forever. He kept thinking of his mother's face as she read Holly's note.

She had written:

Mom,

We are not parcels. We are people. When Dad comes to Great Grandpa's, we'll be there and he can bring us home. We'll open our presents with you tomorrow. Today is our birthday and we don't want to spend it being moved around.

Love,

Holly and Nick

Nick wondered what Mom would do. Would she understand?

How much trouble were they going to be in?

Then the bus turned off the main highway to Guelph and Nick woke his sister. There was no point in worrying. If you were having an adventure, have an adventure.

The trickiest part was phoning Great Grandpa from the bus terminal. Holly would do the talking, of course, but Nick pressed close to give her courage.

"Michael Benson here," Great Grandpa said.

"Hi," Holly began, her voice faint and quavering.

"Speak up," he said. His tone was sharp.

She suddenly could not go on. After a moment, Nick grabbed the receiver, afraid Great Grandpa would hang up.

"It's us, Nick and Holly," he shouted into the phone. "We're at the Guelph bus station. Can you come and get us?"

There was an interminable silence. Then Great Grandpa gave a bark of what might have been laughter or might have been a growl.

"I'll be there in ten minutes," he said and hung up.

The twins sagged with relief. They had to hold each other up. Then they went and sat on a bench to wait.

The jeep pulled up outside the terminal in twelve minutes. Holly and Nick had been watching, so he had no need to fetch them. They were running toward him as though he were Santa Claus himself. He got out and hugged them close. It was the most comforting hug they had had in a long time.

"Happy Birthday, children. Pile in," he said. "You can tell me all about it on the way to the farm."

Holly, her courage completely recovered, told him. He seemed to have already guessed most of it.

"I remember how hard it was for you last year," he said when she stopped to take a breath. "I wanted to help, but they kept telling me to sit down and rest, as though I was too old and feeble to move. You'd be surprised how hard it is sometimes, being old. Do you realize that this is the first time since you were born, that I have been left alone with you?"

They stared at him. It was true.

"It's as though you're a kid, too," Holly said slowly.

"Well, let's make the most of it," Michael Benson chuckled. "Now you've escaped, let's not waste our time together."

Nick, looking at the old man, had a feeling he was keeping something back. He did not guess that, before they had arrived, Great Grandpa had received some frantic phone calls, and had promised the distraught parents that he would let them know if he heard from the children. He had not said he would phone at once, however, and he had no intention of doing so. He meant to let the children have the fun they had worked so hard to get.

The three of them had a sumptuous breakfast. He fried up eggs, bacon, and onions. He cut big slices of the homemade loaf a neighbor had given him, and slathered them with butter and honey from his own bees. Holly and Nick gulped it all down as though they were starving. When they were stuffed to the eyebrows, they groaned and sat back.

"Now, get your duds on," he told them. "I have a cow who's calving. She might have managed alone. But I don't think so. I was with her when you called. I have a phone in the barn now."

As they hiked out to the barnyard, a few first snowflakes began drifting lazily down. The wind sighed through the evergreen trees, "… the only other sound's the sweep of easy wind and downy flake …" Great Grandpa recited.

Holly looked at him, puzzled.

"I know that …" she said uncertainly.

He recited the whole poem. Her face lit up.

"We have it in our reader," she said.

"It's how I feel here," Nick said dreamily. "I never want to go back."

"You will," Great Grandpa said.

Bess, the cow, was giving birth as they came in. It was the most exciting thing the Pennys had ever witnessed. And it went on because she had a second calf a few minutes later. Twins!

"You could call them Holly and Nick," Holly said.

"I could if they weren't both heifers," Great Grandpa chuckled.

Once the twin calves were standing up tipsily on their long spindly legs and having breakfast, Great Grandpa sent the children to collect some evergreen boughs, while he phoned their parents.

There was great jubilation in faraway Toronto.

A multitude of relations began arriving in the late afternoon. As car after car drove in, more snowflakes came spinning down from the dark sky. The family had come laden with a great variety of Christmas edibles. Everyone was in the same house and nobody needed to go anywhere. The presents were opened and there was time for the twins to play with them, while the adults talked and readied the various dishes they had brought for Christmas dinner.

After the eating was over, Aunt Mary went to the piano and they sang carols. Susie, snuggled in her father's arms, slept peacefully. Everyone smiled at her whenever a sleeping baby was mentioned. When the adults began to get ready to go, Grandpa beckoned to Nick and Holly. He led them into the back kitchen and told them softly that he planned to call the calves Happy and Birthday. The twins grinned at him.

"Perfect," Holly whispered.

At last it was time to go. Dad walked a heavy-eyed Nick and a yawning Holly out to Mom's car and tucked them in. They appeared to fall asleep instantly.

"They had the right idea all along," their father said gently, grinning at the seemingly unconscious children.

"I loved it," their mother said. "It was real, wasn't it, David? Not a dream?"

"It was real," he answered, smiling at her.

DO NOT OPEN UNTIL CHRISTMAS

"Next year, let's all start out here," Great Grandpa's voice said, quiet and deep. "I've got room for all of you."

"But Grandpa, you're eighty ..." somebody said.

"So, next year I'll be eighty-one," Great Grandpa said briskly. "But not, I think, dead. If I am, you can make other plans. But get together. Don't drag the children from pillar to post."

Nick and Holly, straining their ears to hear every word, did their best to keep their faces blank.

Then, as their mother headed back to the city, Holly reached out and gave her brother a poke. "We did it," she murmured just loud enough for him to hear.

Nick nodded. The radio was playing "O, come, all ye faithful." As he listened, he caught the word "triumphant."

"That's us," he whispered and tumbled into sleep.

A Present for Miss Potton

Christmas was coming in just nine days. Brian, his brother Chris, and his little sister Robin could hardly wait.

Brian wanted to give his teacher a present. He did not want to give her an ordinary present. He wanted to give her something magnificent.

She never laughed at him the way his parents did, or teased him like his big brother Chris. Even his little sister Robin made fun of him, calling him "silly old Brian."

But Miss Potton smiled at him instead and said, "Well done, Brian," when he got his work right. In her class, he felt special.

Now he wanted, more than anything, to give her a wonderful present.

When the Littles were having supper, Brian told his family what he wished to do.

"Give her a break and skip school," said his big brother Chris. "She'd like that."

Robin stared at Chris. She did not understand what he had just said. Mom and Dad pretended they had not heard.

"How about cookies?" Mom said. "She likes my cookies."

"No," said Brian. "Chico's grandmother is making her cookies."

"Maybe I could make her a pan of fudge," his mother offered.

"No thanks, Mom," Brian told her. "It has to be from me. And I want it to be something truly magnificent."

Dad and Mom smiled. Chris and Robin laughed.

"You're too little," Robin said.

"I am not," said Brian. "You wait and see. I just have to come up with a great idea."

But even though he thought and thought, he could not think of a perfect present for his teacher.

"Line up, children," Miss Potton said the next day. "It's our turn to go and see the big Christmas tree in the library."

The tree was so tall it nearly touched the ceiling. It had lights and tinsel. It had gold balls and a star on the very top.

Miss Potton took a deep breath and smiled.

"It smells like a forest," she said.

Brian sniffed. He had never smelled a forest, but he knew she must be right.

"It's magnificent!" she went on. "I wish we had one like it in our room."

"Me, too," said everyone but Brian. He just smiled. Miss Potton wanted a Christmas tree. Good. He would get her one. A Christmas tree would be perfect.

"Where do you get Christmas trees?" Brian asked his family that night. "Real ones."

"No real trees allowed," Dad said. "It's a Co-op rule."

"Ours looks real," said Mom. "You said you liked it last year, Brian. What's wrong with it?"

"I don't want one for us," Brian told her. "But I need one that smells real. Where do you get them?"

"You buy them at the tree lot," Dad told him.

"Or cut them down," said Chris.

"Chop, chop, BOOM!" Robin shouted.

Everyone but Brian laughed. The next day was Saturday. When nobody was watching, Brian shook his piggy bank. Two dimes, two quarters, and one loony fell out. Would that be enough?

He hoped so. He put on his snowsuit and boots. He walked to the tree lot near the church. He held out his money to the man who was selling the trees.

"Is this enough for a tree?" he asked.

The man grinned and shook his head.

"Sorry, son," he said. "Real trees cost real money."

Brian trudged home, thinking hard. He could not buy a tree for his teacher. But he would get her one somehow. He must.

Brian got his toy axe. He went up the hill behind the Co-op. He did not see any big trees there. He only saw little ones. He stopped to look at them.

"You are too small," he told them. "Miss Potton wants a big one. Keep on growing, little trees."

He walked on. He looked and looked. It was late. He was tired. But he kept looking.

At last, he found a beautiful one in front of a big house. It stood tall and it smelled like a forest.

"You are just right," he told it. "Miss Potton will love you."

Brian swung his toy axe at the trunk as hard as he could. The head flew off. The blade left no mark whatsoever on the tree.

Brian went for Chris's hatchet. It was bigger. He tried again. He swung it three times before it broke, too. He was glad Chris did not bother with it any longer, so he would not mind. Not much, anyway.

Brian sat down on the snow. He thought and thought. But he could not think of any other way to get a tree for Miss Potton. He wanted to cry.

Then a van drove up. A tree stuck out of it. Brian jumped up and went to look at the tree.

It was big. It was beautiful. It smelled like a forest.

A man got out and smiled at Brian.

"How do you like our tree?" he asked.

"I like it a lot," Brian told him. "I need one just like it."

"Come by on Monday," the man said. "We got the tree for our Christmas party. But we're going south as soon as it's over. After the party, we'll throw out this tree. You can help yourself."

"Wow! Thanks a lot," Brian said.

He flew home. On Monday, he'd get up early and he'd take the tree to his teacher. It would be a magnificent present. It would be perfect, and it would be from him. He could hardly wait.

He did not tell his family about the tree he had found. They would laugh at him. All weekend, he kept watch outside the big house. Through the front window, he could see them putting up the tree. He watched them put lights and balls and tinsel on it. They put a star on the top. When people started coming to the party, he went home.

Before it was light on Monday morning, Brian woke his mother and told her he had to go to school early. She was too sleepy to ask questions. He ran all the way to the big house. The tree lay by the road. The star was gone. So were the lights and gold balls.

But it still smelled like a forest. Brian took hold of the trunk. He tugged. He pulled. He pulled. He tugged. The tree did not move. It was too heavy for him to shift.

Brian almost gave up. Then he thought of Miss Potton. She wanted a tree so much.

He ran home.

"I need you," he told Chris. Robin came, too. Then he got Josh and Chico and Sarah and Amy.

Brian told them about the tree. Robin's eyes got big.

"Chop, chop, BOOM?" she asked.

"No. Listen." Brian told them what the man had said and that the tree was for Miss Potton.

"Okay, let's go," said Chris.

When they saw the tree, they gasped. Then they all tugged and pulled. They pulled and tugged. The tree shifted a tiny bit. Then, just as they were going to give up, it began to slide over the snow.

"Way to go," yelled Brian.

They dragged the tree across the park. When they started to pull it across the street, cars stopped for them.

"It's sure heavy," puffed Chris. But he kept pulling.

"It's getting slush and dirt on it," Josh said. "And bits are breaking off."

"Never mind. The top side is fine," said Brian.

They got to the school at last. Brian stood by his tree. Sarah ran for Miss Potton.

"Don't say why," Brian told Sarah.

Everyone waited. At last, they heard Miss Potton coming.

"What is it, Sarah?" she was saying. "I'm very busy."

Then she saw all the children. And she saw the big tree.

"Oh, my!" said Brian's teacher.

"Brian found it for you," said Chris. "I'll take Robin home now. If I don't hurry, I'll be late."

The children brushed off the dirt and water with their mitts. The janitor carried the tree to Miss Potton's room. The one side was a mess. But they stood it in the corner so only the good side showed.

"Are you surprised, Miss Potton?" Chico asked.

"I am, I am," Miss Potton said. Then she took a deep breath. "It smells like a forest."

"It needs lights," said Brian. "And tinsel and a star on top."

"Then let's get busy," said his teacher.

The class made beautiful things for the tree. They brought things from home, too. The janitor came in with a string of lights.

Brian drew the star and cut it out with great care. Then he sprayed it with sparkles.

"That is a splendid star, Brian," his teacher said. She strung a wire through it to attach it to the top of the tree. When it was ready, she held the ladder while Brian climbed up and fastened it onto the very top.

When he had climbed down again, the teacher stood and gazed at the tree.

"I don't know how you did it, Brian," she said. "It is lovely."

Brian blushed. He felt he would burst with pride. He had done it. He had given Miss Potton a perfect present.

Then he remembered how the others had helped him.

"A man let me have it," he said. "Then the others all pitched in and got it here."

Miss Potton laughed.

"Brian Little," she said, "you are like this tree."

Brian stared at her.

"Me? Like the tree?" he asked. "How?"

"Your best side is showing," his teacher told him, "and you are truly magnificent."

Do Not Open Until Christmas

When Will woke up, it was still dark but he knew it was morning. That wasn't all he knew. Before he opened his eyes, he knew it was Christmas.

He rolled over and poked his dog.

"Hey, Snuggles, it's Christmas," he told her.

Snug yawned but she kept her eyes shut. She had not finished sleeping. She knew they weren't going to get up yet. She was not a bouncing puppy who jumped up the minute her master stirred. She was ten and she needed her rest.

"Oh, Snug, do wake up," Will said, poking her harder. "I got you a present. If you get up, I can give it to you right now."

He slid out of bed and shivered. It was cold in his bedroom. He snatched up a thick sweatshirt and pulled it on over his head.

Snug had finally opened her eyes. She had not moved from her warm spot deep in his covers, but she was watching him. And he could tell that her curly tail had begun to quiver.

"Come on," he said, "but keep quiet. Mom said we couldn't get up until it was light outside."

Snug sighed and thumped down onto the floor. If Will was leaving, she would have to go, too. Keeping an eye on the boy was her job.

Will crept down the stairs. Snug sighed and padded after him. When the two of them got to the bottom without waking anyone, the boy led the way to the living room. When he flicked the switch, the tree lights came on. He grinned. They were so bright, and turning them on was like waving a wand. The ordinary room was suddenly magical.

And piled high under the evergreen's branches were the presents!

He stared at them eagerly. Not that he was going to open them. Not yet. It was far too early. But nobody would care if he gave Snug hers ahead of time.

But where was it? He had wrapped it and left it right on top when he went to bed. But someone must have moved things.

He tiptoed over to the tree and went down on his knees to search for it. He didn't mean to examine any other packages. But he had to shift some to find his gift for the dog.

The first one he lifted up was the one he had been staring at ever since his mother had put it there, the day before yesterday. It was big and heavy and, when he had shaken it gently, it had made just the noise he wanted to hear. Lego rattling! He shook it again. Was it the Lego castle he so longed to put together? He had shown it to his mother when they had been in Simply Wonderful.

One corner of the wrapping paper was slightly torn. He eased it open a little more. Then, before he could stop himself, his hands had ripped the paper completely off, and he was right. It was exactly the one he wanted. She had only pretended not to notice.

He tried to put the wrapping paper back onto the box, but it was impossible. He pushed the present back behind other things and saw his own name on another parcel, a smaller one that had an interesting shape. This time, opening it was partly Snug's fault. She jumped at it when he held it up and it was her paws that started removing the paper. It was a flashlight that had all sorts of special features, in case you got lost in the wilderness: a compass, a beeping signal, a knife. It was from his grandmother.

"She's not here so she won't care that I opened it," he told the dog. "Besides, it's mine. So I can open it early if I like."

He knew they would be mad at him, though. He had better find Snug's new toy and get out of here before he got caught.

He found it finally and dug it out. She knew it was hers the moment he put it down in front of her. While she was ripping off the paper this time, he saw another one for him. It was from his mother. When he squeezed the package, he knew it was something to wear.

Pajamas, probably. She had said he needed some. He dropped it and picked up one more, which turned out to be a book he had been wanting to read. He tried not to reach for any more but, by now, he could not resist.

He had almost everything meant for him opened when he suddenly saw, outside the window, the light of morning. And then, before he could make a run for it, he heard them coming. They were singing "O, come, all ye faithful" and they sounded happy.

But his mother stopped singing at the bottom of the stairs.

"Where's Will? Will!" she called. "Wait, everybody. We can't start without Will."

But his sister Dora had not waited. She stood in the doorway, staring at him.

She was puzzled at first, and then her face filled with fury.

"He's here," she shouted, "and he's opened all the presents. He's ruined Christmas."

Hearing the shocked disgust in her voice, Will cringed. She didn't have to be so mean. He snatched Snug into his arms and held her in front of him like a shield.

"I did not," he yelled back. "Shut up, Dora. They're all mine. I could do what I liked with my own things."

Then his parents were there and the horrible moment arrived. His mother stared at him and then sank down on the couch and began to cry.

Dora ran and wrapped her arms around Mom's neck, giving her a comforting hug.

Will could not move. He was angry and ashamed. He hadn't touched anyone else's things, he reminded himself. Why was Mom so upset? Why was his sister such a goody-goody? What could he do to fix things?

Dad helped. He put on some Christmas music and he handed out the stockings, which Will had not even remembered. Soon they were opening the other gifts as well. They did not look at Will, but they did not keep on scolding. At last, Dad handed Mom the parcel from Will.

He had chosen the mittens inside it with great care. They exactly matched her eyes and they were wonderfully soft and warm. He was sure she would love wearing them.

And watching her beginning to open the gift was like getting a gift himself. She tore the paper off. Then she slid her hands into them and held them against her cheeks. She looked across at him and smiled.

"They're lovely, Will," she said in a voice that shook a bit. "Thank you."

And then he understood what he had done. He had taken away from everyone their joy in seeing people getting the gifts they had chosen for them. His mother had missed seeing his delight in the Lego castle.

He had not said anything, except for mumbling "Thank you" every so often. But now he stood up and took a step toward the couch. Before he could get to his mother, however, Snug got in the way and, suddenly, Will tumbled head over heels and landed upside down in the big carton they were using to put the ripped wrapping paper in.

Dora broke into a fit of giggles. Snug tried to jump in with her master. Mom began to ask if he was hurt and choked back a chuckle before she could get the words out.

"Shall I throw him out, or do you suppose he's a present for you, dear?" his father said, gripping Will by his ankles and pulling him upright.

Will felt like crying, at first, and then was astonished to find himself joining in the uproar the rest of them were making. It wasn't funny, and yet he could not stop.

And then, all at once, he knew what to do next.

He pushed Snug away and dove under the tree to get the last package, the one he had not bothered with. There was a sticker on it saying *Do Not Open Until Christmas*. Well, he hadn't. And he had been right about it being clothes.

It wasn't pajamas but a large sweatshirt with a picture of a pug dog on the front. Will held it up and looked at his mother.

"Oh, Mom," he croaked, "it is ... just what I wanted. It is perfect. Thank you—and I'm sorry."

She smiled at him, her eyes filled with love.

"I knew you'd be thrilled," she said. "Merry Christmas, son."

And, pulling his new shirt on, Will knew that Christmas wasn't ruined, whatever his sister said. Wrecking something as old and tough as Christmas was impossible. This Christmas was the day for letting Dora help him build his Lego castle.

One of the Family

Thomas was lifting his first spoonful of cereal to his mouth, when his foster mother Julie said, "Just think, Thomas. When you go to bed tonight, you will have a mother, a father, a sister, and a little brother. It will be so wonderful for you to spend Christmas with a family all your own. You must be excited."

Thomas bent his head so he would not have to meet her eyes, and he shoved the cereal into his mouth so he would not have to reply. He wasn't excited. He was scared.

He had met the Browns, of course, so they weren't total strangers. He had been to their house twice, and he had gone to the butterfly place with Miranda and her dad. But he hadn't slept over, and he had always known he was coming back to Julie's.

He couldn't explain all this to her. And he couldn't tell her he had been remembering his real mother a lot lately.

"If you don't want the rest of that cereal, leave it," Julie told him. "How about a piece of toast and peanut butter?"

Thomas pushed back his bowl and nodded his head.

He had never known his father. Mom had just said he had walked out on them, and Thomas should be thankful. But Thomas knew his mother had loved him. He remembered her cradling him on her lap and singing to him. He remembered the feel of her hand holding his tightly as they crossed the street. She had yelled at him sometimes, and they had been hard up for money, but they had managed until she got sick.

"You'd better leave that bite and finish getting ready, boy," Julie told him, breaking in on his memories. "Carlotta will be here any minute."

When Thomas heard the social worker's car turn into the driveway, he had just finished cleaning his glasses. He put them back on and tried to ignore the queasy feeling in his stomach.

"Thomas," Julie called, "she's here. Come quick and let me give you a fast inspection."

Thomas could not get words past the lump in his throat, but he ran to where she waited. He had his new jacket and boots on. He only needed to put his hat on and find some mitts.

"Here's your hat," Julie said, smiling at him. "And here's a present I made for you."

She was holding out the pair of scarlet mittens he had watched her knitting the week before. He had wondered if they were to be his Christmas present, but he had tried not to let her see his interest. Now, catching sight of his initials on the backs, he understood why she had flipped them over whenever he came near. He grinned at her and tried to find the words to tell her how much he liked them. Before he could, they both heard Carlotta coming up the outside steps.

"I know you like them," Julie said, laughing softly. "Put them on while I let Carlotta in."

Thomas gulped and pulled on the first mitt. He tried to feel excited. But instead, he felt the way he had on the first day at school, small and anxious. Julie gave him a big hug as he was about to get into the car.

Maybe Carlotta guessed, because she did not waste any time chatting.

"Let's go, Thomas," she said. "You bring that backpack and I'll take the bags. He looks great, Julie."

He ran to the Children's Aid car and scrambled into the back seat. He peered at his reflection in the rear-view mirror. His dark hair was tucked out of sight under his new cap. His eyes, partly hidden by the glasses, were such a dark brown that they were almost black. He tried smiling at himself but he couldn't. He stuck out his tongue, then pulled it back in before Carlotta could see, and felt braver.

"I'll bet you're excited, Thomas," the social worker said.

Thomas wished they would all stop talking about how he felt. He nodded. But he turned his head so she could not guess how uptight he was. The Browns were nice. He had liked them when he visited at their house. But today was different.

"I'll bet you go to the Santa Claus Parade on Sunday," Carlotta went on. She was sounding so cheerful that Thomas longed to cover his ears.

Then the car started to slow down.

"Here we are," she said. He watched her waving to somebody. Probably Mom. That was what Mrs. Brown said he should call her.

He peered down the snowy walk. He had guessed right. His new mother was pulling on her coat and hurrying out to meet them. Now she was smiling in at him and opening the car door.

"Welcome to your new home, Thomas," she said, holding out both hands to him.

Thomas shrank back in the car. He had taken off his new mittens. He dropped one on purpose and took his time bending down to retrieve it. He was not ready to be one of the Browns quite yet.

"What great mittens!" Mom said, shoving her hands into her pockets.

He looked at her then.

"Julie made them for me," he told her.

Then a voice called, "Mommy, make him get out."

It was Miranda. Thomas could not see her but he knew her voice.

She must be hiding behind her mother. He liked Miranda. He laughed and slid past his new mother. Hearing her helped him relax. Where was she?

Mom turned and said, "Go back inside, Miranda, or you'll freeze. We'll be there in a minute."

She was still smiling but she sounded cross.

Thomas stepped around her and looked for his new sister. There she was. She was grinning and prancing about in the snow. She had on boots that were way too big for her. She had wrapped a long scarf around herself and perched a straw hat on her head. Her mother tried to catch hold of her but Miranda dodged out of reach and laughed.

"Andy is scared to come out," she told Thomas. "He says you're too big."

Andy was Miranda's little brother. He was not yet three years old and small for his age.

"I'm not so big," Thomas said.

"Miranda Brown," her mother snapped. "You march yourself right back into the house. Andrew is not scared. He is just excited about his new brother coming."

Miranda clumped a few steps up the walk. The boots slipped and slid in the fresh snow. Thomas thought they must be her father's.

"Come on, new brother," she shouted.

Thomas wondered if Andy was really scared. He followed Miranda to the house. Carlotta and Mom came behind them. He could hear the two women talking as though they had known each other forever. Mom was helping to carry his stuff.

He watched Miranda stamp up to the door. He was sure her boots would fall off any minute.

His new boots fitted him perfectly. All the clothes he was wearing were new. Julie said he should be dressed for his new life in a new outfit, new from the skin out and from top to toe.

"Your celebration suit," she had called it. Even his undershirt and boxer shorts were new. Julie had washed them so they wouldn't itch, but they still felt strange.

Once they were all inside, Miranda hopped around, kicking off the big boots and letting the scarf slide to the floor.

"That is Aunt Sally's gardening hat, miss," Mom told her daughter, lifting the straw hat off her tumbled hair and hanging it back on its hook.

Miranda giggled.

"Aunt Silly wouldn't mind," she declared. "She told me it suited me."

Mom sighed.

"She would," she replied, looking at Carlotta and shrugging her shoulders.

Thomas ignored them. He was trying to find Andy. Then he saw him. His new little brother was hiding behind a big chair. Thomas guessed he did not know that his feet showed underneath. Andy's new brother laughed.

Miranda looked to see what was so funny. Then she laughed, too.

"Oh, Andy, what a nut you are!" she teased the little boy.

"Am not a nut!" Andy yelled and came out from behind the chair. He stared at Thomas for a moment and then ran to his mother.

Thomas took off his hat and stuffed his new mitts into his pockets. Then he sat down on the floor to pull off his boots.

Carlotta came over and smiled down at him.

"I have to go to work," she said, "but I'll be back at suppertime. They've invited me to your welcoming party."

Thomas was unzipping his coat. He glanced up and muttered, "Bye."

"See you later," Mom told her.

Thomas heard a scurrying sound from the space under the couch. He stopped pulling off his coat and got down flat on his tummy. He peered into the darkness and listened.

"What are you doing?" Miranda demanded.

"Hush," he told her. "There's someone under here."

"Someone!" Miranda shrieked and landed next to him.

There was a small scrabbling sound and then a silence. It was as though someone was holding his breath. Then Thomas heard a sneeze so small it made him laugh.

"It's a chipmunk," Miranda whispered into his ear.

"Where is he?" Thomas started to ask. Then he saw a tiny shadow hunched into the corner, a small creature with eyes like bright beads.

"What on earth are you two doing?" Miranda's mother asked.

"Chip," Andy told her.

Then the chipmunk darted to the other corner, looking for a way out.

"Hey, little guy," Thomas murmured. "Don't be scared. We won't hurt you."

Miranda backed up and scrambled to her feet.

"Mommy, it's true. There's a little chipmunk under the couch," she said, so excited that her words tumbled over each other. "He's scared silly."

The chipmunk was now running back and forth.

"Leave him be for a moment," Mom said softly. "Maybe he will come out. If he's a chipmunk, he might be friendly. When we were at Miranda's aunt's cottage, Thomas, one ate out of our hands. Maybe we should put some nuts down to coax him."

Thomas was just wondering where they would find some nuts, when Miranda ran out and was back in no time with peanuts.

"Move over, Thomas," she said.

Thomas got up slowly. He did not want to desert his new friend. He wanted to comfort him. But Miranda was the one with the nuts.

Then they all heard the front door close. Dad was home. Thomas wanted to be the one to tell him about the chipmunk, but he was too shy. He waited.

"Good morning, Thomas. What's going on?" Dad asked.

Miranda was lying on the floor, her bottom up, spreading the peanuts out on the carpet in front of the couch.

Thomas cleared his throat and said, "There's a chipmunk under there."

His new father grinned.

"There's a hippopotamus in the garden," he said, as if Thomas was joking.

"I'm not kidding," Thomas insisted. "Miranda is coaxing him out with nuts."

Mom had gone to the front door and opened it wide.

"If we all sit down and keep still," she said, "maybe he will make a dash for freedom."

They were just getting seated when the chipmunk shot across the rug, into the hall, and straight out the open door. He had two peanuts bulging out of his little face, and Thomas thought he looked very pleased with himself.

"You weren't kidding, Thomas. I apologize," Dad said, sitting down.

Thomas's eyes met his new father's. He took two steps toward the man and hesitated. Dad reached out a long arm and pulled him onto his knee.

"Hey, Tom Tom," he said, "how's your first day being a brother?"

Held fast, Thomas felt happiness well up inside him. He leaned his head against his father's shoulder and said, "I think I'll like it."

Andy had run to the door to wave.

"Bye bye, chip," they heard him call.

"If we put the rest of the nuts out on the porch, I'll bet he'll come back for them," Mom said. "You take care of it, Miranda, while I get us some lunch."

"And when we've finished, I'm going to take Miranda and Thomas on an expedition. When Andy gets up from his nap, we'll have a grand surprise waiting for him," Dad told them.

He would not explain. When Miranda and Thomas were in the car, they still had no idea where they were going. Miranda kept saying, "Just tell us if it is a present for Andy, or if Thomas and I get one, too," but Dad would not give in to her pleading. Thomas did not ask. He did not think it would be a present. Presents would come on Christmas, and it was just a few days away.

But now, he thought with a smile, if Julie asked me, I could say I am excited.

Then the car slowed down and Miranda let out a cheer. They were at a Christmas tree lot.

As they got out and began patrolling the rows of fragrant evergreens, Thomas felt like skipping. He had never before been to buy a real tree. He could not remember Christmases before he lived at Julie's, and her tree came out of a box.

"I get to pick," Miranda said loudly, "because I'm a girl and I'm younger."

"Miranda," her father began.

"I don't mind her choosing," Thomas said.

He was not looking at the tree Miranda clearly wanted. It was tall and straight and practically perfect. But he was staring down at a chunky little tree with a hole in its trunk. It had lots of branches and looked not at all noble.

"Dad," he paused for a moment. Then he blurted, "Could we get this one for the chipmunk?"

"Chipmunks don't have Christmas trees," Miranda scoffed.

Thomas realized that Dad was looking at him steadily. "We could put it outside and hang stuff on it," Thomas told him. "We could string some nuts together and prunes maybe, and ..."

"We'll get both," Dad told the man who was grinning at Thomas.

"He's our new brother," Miranda explained to the man. "That's why my dad is spoiling him. Even though he is being dumb."

"I think you had better get in the car, Miranda," her father said. "Can you carry your tree, Thomas?"

Miranda's shoulders had drooped and she was trudging toward the place where the car was parked. She looked so sad that Thomas felt like running to hug her.

"I can if Miranda helps me," he said, grabbing one of the thicker branches in his red mittens and beginning to tug the little tree away from the fence where it was leaning.

"Wait. I'm coming," Miranda sang out. She bolted past her father and grabbed hold of the next branch over.

"Thanks," she whispered.

Thomas started puffing. The little tree was heavier than he had expected. When they reached the car, Dad was waiting with the trunk open. He smiled at them and leaned down to heave the chipmunk's tree in.

"We'll tie the other one on the roof," he told the man selling the trees.

"Sure," the man said, still grinning at Thomas's choice.

Mom and Andy were bundled up, playing in the snow, when the car drove up. They rushed to see what the other three had brought home. Mom stared at Miranda's choice, lashed onto the car roof.

"It's gorgeous," she said. "It even has a perfect point for the star."

"Wait till you see the one Thomas chose," her daughter giggled.

"Blame it on your son," Dad said.

Thomas saw her glance down at Andy, who was holding onto her leg.

"The other one, Josieann," Dad said, giving her a straight look.

Thomas saw Mom's confusion. It only lasted a second, but he wished Dad had not mixed her up. It was her first day having two boys.

"Look here, Mommy," Miranda shouted gleefully, tugging her to where she could see the squat little tree inside. "Thomas wants it for the chipmunk."

Mom understood instantly. She beamed at Thomas.

"I'll bet he'll love it," she said.

"We can string nuts and fruit. I'm sure he'd like slices of the little oranges," Thomas explained. He had started speaking shyly, but the more ideas he had, the more excited his voice became.

"Can we do the chippie's tree first?" Miranda wanted to know.

"Of course," her mother said. "Let's go and find some things he'd like, while your father gets it standing up."

"I thought we could tie it next to the cranberry bush," Dad said.

They got busy. Even Andy helped. They made popcorn balls stuck together with corn syrup. They threaded pieces of dried apple and apricots on strings. Dad brought out a skinny carrot and some raw apples cut in quarters.

"No tinsel," Mom said. "It might choke them. We'd better get the big tree inside before supper. Remember we have guests coming. Carlotta and Julie will soon be arriving. It's a good thing the food is in the oven already."

Thomas had forgotten. His eyes shone. Julie, he knew, would love his chipmunk tree. As he headed for the house, he turned his head and whispered, "Merry Christmas, chippy."

Julie did love their tree. Carlotta took lots of pictures of it. Supper was yummy, too, and for dessert, there was a splendid cake with one big candle.

"That's to celebrate your first day," Mom told him

"Happy first day to you," Miranda began to sing, and everyone joined in.

Then the company left. Mom took Andy onto her lap for his bedtime story. The little boy looked over at Thomas, who was watching them.

"Tom, come," he said.

"Good idea," Mom said, patting the couch next to her. Thomas went and sat close enough to see the pictures. *Wombat Divine* and *Pippin the Christmas Pig*. Reading them together that way made Thomas feel warm and Christmassy.

Before long, it was bedtime for the older children. Thomas put on the new pajamas Julie had given him. When he started to clamber into his bed, he saw, at the head, his own special pillow, the one he had always used at Julie's. She must have brought it with her. He snuggled into it, sniffing the smell that put him to sleep.

Then Mom came in.

"Well, how was it—your first day of being a brother?" she asked, leaning down to push his hair out of his eyes.

He remembered his real mother doing that. He did not answer this one's question. Instead, he asked one of his own. "Do you think my chipmunk will come back in the morning?"

"I do," she said.

"Being a brother is great," he said then, giving a giant yawn.

She pulled the covers up to his chin and went over to the window.

"Oh, my!" she said then. "Thomas, come here. Quietly."

He slid out of bed and tiptoed across to stand next to her. The moon was full and the snow shone. He saw a shadow move. His eyes widened. There, at the foot of the short, chunky tree, a small animal was having a bedtime snack. It had a tail, so it wasn't his chipmunk, but he didn't mind.

"Shh," she warned him. "I think it's a raccoon. Chipmunks sleep at night. But you've given it a fine feast."

He hesitated. Then he spoke softly.

"Let's get Miranda," he said.

At that moment, Dad stuck his head in the door and Mom whispered, "David, bring Miranda. Quietly. There's a raccoon at Thomas's tree."

Thomas held his breath as his new father tiptoed away. The raccoon lifted his head for an instant but, seeing no danger threatening, he went back for another helping. Then Dad was next to them, carrying a sleepy Miranda in his arms. Keeping still, the four of them gazed out the window, spellbound at the sight of the small creature who had come to have his Christmas dinner with them.

And Thomas, leaning against his mother, knew he wasn't just a guest now. He was one of the family. And he was at home.

The Boy Who Didn't Believe in Christmas

Everyone said that this was going to be a green Christmas but, when December was half over, the first real snow finally arrived. There had been a flurry or two earlier but the flakes had melted in minutes. Then, at last, Luke and his big sister Elspeth wakened to see a white world outside their bedroom windows. When Luke got to the kitchen, Elspeth was dancing their mother around the breakfast table.

"Yippee!" she cheered. "A white Christmas! We can go skiing."

Before this, Luke had always loved the first snow as much as she did. But now, he stared at the fat flakes drifting lazily down and scowled.

"I don't believe in Christmas," he muttered, jerking out his chair and sitting down.

"Don't be dumb," Elspeth snapped. "Anyway, who cares what you believe. You don't have to think Santa Claus is real to have fun opening your presents. What I want more than anything this year is an iPhone. They are so cool."

Luke did not bother listening to her. He knew already that he would not get the things he wanted. He longed for the latest Call of Duty game his friend Barry had. His mother said he could not have it because it was filled with terrible violence. She was sure it would turn him into a killer.

"Barry's father plays it," he had argued. "Are you saying he's a killer? He's a policeman, Mom."

She said she was not responsible for Barry's father, just for her son Luke. And he would not get the game from her.

He wanted a gun, too. Not a baby toy one, but one that looked real and actually worked. But his father said even toy guns were dangerous if they looked real. People seeing him with one might panic and overreact. Definitely no gun!

And he wanted a dog, of course. He had wanted a dog ever since he could remember. But Elspeth's stupid cat, Jemima, who was given to her before Luke was old enough to speak up for dogs, was supposedly terrified of them, and that was that.

What was the point of Christmas if you never got what you really wanted?

For Christmases in the past, they got him stuff, of course.

Books. A computer game that helped you make cartoons. A big mug with his name on it! It was getting that dumb mug, and hearing his mother blather on about how she had to shop for "stocking stuffers," that were the last straws. Why bother hanging up stockings for Santa to fill, when everybody knew his mother got the small presents, and she and Dad stuffed the stockings after he was in bed? It was dumb.

He gobbled his toast and went to get dressed.

It was a school day. He thought they should declare it a Snow Day, but he knew they would not. As soon as he had shoved his homework into his backpack, he put on his jacket and headed into the wintry morning. The thought of being shut inside an overheated classroom, watching the snow falling on the other side of the tall blank windows, was dismal. When he had been younger and still believed in Christmas, their teachers had decorated the classroom with snowmen and holly wreaths. But now, they were supposed to be too old for such things, he supposed, and the undecorated windows matched the empty darkness inside him.

"Jinga-jing, jinga-jing!" a voice sang.

Luke spun around and grinned at the little girl in the wheelchair. Her name was Polly Charles and she was one of his favorite people in all the world. She was being pushed by her grandfather, and she was bundled up to the eyes in layers of clothes to keep out the cold.

"Hi, Mr. Charles," Luke said. "Hi, Polly."

He waited for her head to turn slowly toward him and said "Hi" again once their eyes met.

"Jinga-jing!" Polly sang proudly.

Luke squatted down next to her. Then he sang "Jingle Bells" softly, making each word sound out clearly.

She tried to clap, but her arms were swaddled in wool and she had to nod instead. The tassel on her knitted cap bobbed up and down with each jerk of her head and made them all laugh.

"It's snowing, Polly," he said then. He scooped up a few flakes and held them close to her warm cheek.

He wanted to see her eyes light up. But she just gazed at him and nodded her head up and down again to make the tassel bounce some more.

One thing was for sure, Christmas meant nothing special to Polly. The Sunday school had given her a doll and a bag of candies the year before, but she couldn't play with a doll, and her grandfather was afraid she would choke on one of the hard toffees. His mother had bought her a sweater, he remembered, but clothes weren't what kids Polly's age longed for.

Somebody should figure out the right present for her, he thought. But what?

"You haven't time to hang around dreaming of a white Christmas, boy," Polly's grandfather told him. "If you don't get a move on, you'll be late."

"I'll make it," Luke said. "But I'm not dreaming about Christmas. I don't believe in it anymore."

"Nonsense," the old man said, pulling his coat tighter around himself and taking hold of the wheelchair handles again. Glancing down, Luke saw that he wore no gloves and his fingers were red with cold.

"So long, Poll," he called to the child, and he began to race down the wet sidewalk.

He could not keep his mind on schoolwork that morning. Over and over, his thoughts returned to Mr. Charles's cold hands and thin coat.

When his thoughts turned to Polly, Luke wracked his brain for a present he could give her that she would care about. Even though her laugh was loud and a bit hoarse, it was real in a way Elspeth's wasn't. It held such delight in the bobbing tassel and the one word she had learned to sing.

Then his class went to Assembly for a presentation about saving water. He knew it mattered but he hardly listened. Once the teacher's helper brought Justin in, he gave up completely on the subject of water and watched Justin.

The teacher had never explained what was wrong with Justin, but Luke's mother had told him. She worked with Justin's mother at the shop. Justin was autistic.

"Autistic and weird," Elspeth had said. "I mean, what's with him? His cousin told me he has a pie pan he spins, and he just sits there, spinning it and watching for hours."

Mom had given them a big lecture on autism after that. She said Justin might be very bright. His mother was sure he was. But he had trouble connecting with people. He also made noises that disturbed the class and then, each time, he was led away by the teacher's assistant.

I bet he doesn't believe in Christmas, either, Luke thought, watching the boy staring at one of the brass buttons on his jacket as though it was magical.

When they were marching out of the Assembly Hall, Luke passed the kid and said, "Hi, Justin."

The boy's eyes skidded across Luke's face and away without pausing.

"Come along, Justin," the woman with him said loudly. She sounded as though she were talking to a dog. Luke watched him being tugged away and hated her.

Then he saw Barry twirl his finger next to his temple. Luke scowled at him.

"What's with you and the weirdo?" Barry asked, sounding surprised.

Luke opened his mouth to answer and then shut it. What could he say? He pretended he had not heard. His friend would think he was nuts. But he still wished he understood what Justin was thinking. As Justin's gaze had sped over his face, Luke had seen somebody looking out.

He pushed the idea away.

"Barry, tell me," he asked. "Do you believe in Christmas?"

"Do I!" Barry said, grinning. "I've given my dad a list and my mom another. Kids whose parents are divorced get twice the loot, you know. And the parents feel so guilty, they try to out-do each other. It's great, man. Too bad yours don't split."

He roared with laughter. Then he turned to talk to Cindy March. She was pretending he did not exist. Then the bell rang for break. He knew better than to tell his friend that he felt sorry for him. But he did. Barry didn't have a proper home anymore. He was always being shipped from one parent to the other. Luke was not crazy about Elspeth, but he still wanted one home, with a sister and two parents in it.

Two days later, he found the spinning top he had put away with the other little things he had got at the Christmas party his family had had the year before. It had come from his grandmother. She had had it forever. She showed him how to spin it and he had played with it for ages. As soon as he saw it in the carton, he knew who would love it.

But it was not bright, just dull brown. He was shoving it back when he was inspired. Hiding it deep in his pocket, he went to Elspeth's room. She was in the living room, playing music and dancing with her friend Sonia. He probably had plenty of time to get the stuff. If only she had silver!

She did. The tiny bottle was half empty but he thought there was plenty.

Half an hour later, the surface of the spinning top was painted with silver nail polish. He replaced the almost empty bottle and took one with a little scarlet left. With great care, he added a bright line underneath. Then he blew on it until it was dry. At last, just to make sure, he propped it up against the Kleenex box on his dresser and left it.

He wandered back out to the living room, trying to decide whether to give Justin the top at school or take it over to his house. He didn't really want Barry or any of the others to see him presenting the top to the boy, but it wasn't only that. He had a feeling Justin might not understand what the top was for if he was given it at school.

Also, Luke did not want the teacher's helper to be watching. She gushed over Justin when people were around, but Luke had seen her roll her eyes when he didn't do what she said, and sometimes she could be rough with him. She would make a big scene over the toy top. He could picture it perfectly.

"Oh, Justin, honey, look what your friend Luke has brought for you. How sweet!"

That settled the question. He'd take the top over to the house.

He was about to set out with it hidden in his pocket the next afternoon, when Elspeth caught him.

"Would you do me a favor, little brother?" she cooed.

 DO NOT OPEN UNTIL CHRISTMAS

"I doubt it," he said. Then, catching sight of her expression, he asked, "What favor?"

"I want to buy Jemima a Christmas present," she told him, holding out a ten-dollar bill. "But I can't take the time right now. I want to get her a new collar. If you'll go for me, you can keep the change. They are having a sale at Pet-Purree, but I think it ends tonight."

She went on explaining but he could not be bothered paying attention. She knew he liked visiting the pet store. Sometimes they had great puppies. He liked the parrots, too.

"Okay, okay," he growled. Pretending to be mad. "Gimme the money. Are you sure this is enough?"

She added another ten and beamed at him as he jogged out the door.

At the pet shop, he examined the cat collars. A lady standing by the counter picked one up and shook it. Tiny bells rang. Luke stared at it and then grinned.

"How much?" he asked.

He could not believe it. He could afford two of them, plus the tax. Perfect.

"Jinga-jing, jinga-jing," he sang under his breath as he headed for Justin's.

Luck was with him. Justin's brother let him in. He gave Luke a funny look, but he told him Justin was in the den downstairs. Luke thanked him and ran down. He felt uneasy as he looked at the boy, who was spinning a pie plate, just as Elspeth had said.

"Hey, Justin," he said. "Look at this."

Justin did not look at first. But then the little top flashed in the light and his attention was caught. Luke held onto the small toy until he thought the other boy knew how to make it go. Then he let him take it. He waited, watching. The pie plate lay forgotten as Justin spun the little silver top across the floor.

"Who did you say wanted him?" an adult voice asked.

Luke got up and started for the stairs. As he began to climb, he turned back for a second.

"Merry Christmas, Justin," he said.

Justin glanced up but only for an instant. Then he returned to spinning the top.

As Luke left the house, he felt great. He bent down, scooped up a handful of the snow, and sent a snowball flying at the nearest tree trunk.

Once he reached home, he was careful to put the cat collar with the bells away in his underwear drawer. The other one had one big bell and would be fine for old Jemima. After all, she was not a kitten. Elspeth had had her for nine years.

He found his sister in the hall closet, head down in the big box of winter mittens and scarves they handed out when friends came without what they needed to keep warm, while tobogganing or making a snow person. As she straightened up and took the cat collar from him, he looked into the contents of the Mitten Trunk. There, before his very eyes, was a pair of warm gloves that used to belong to his father.

"Good show," Luke said and snatched them up. He was absolutely sure they would fit Mr. Charles. There was probably a scarf that would be good, too, but he did not want the old man to refuse to take the things. One pair of gloves would be just what the doctor ordered.

"Those are too big for you, dummy," Elspeth said.

"I'll grow into them," Luke answered, smirking.

Then he raced up to his room before she quizzed him any further.

As they finished supper, the doorbell rang. It was Polly's grandfather. He wondered if Luke would be free to help him take Polly to the carol service at the church on Christmas Eve. Getting her chair up the stairs was not easy.

"Sure," Luke said.

"I thought you were going to the party Barry's mother …" his sister started in.

"You thought wrong," Luke said firmly. He turned to Mr. Charles. "I'll come over early so we will have lots of time."

"Good boy," the old man said and left.

"You realize it will be a Christmas service," Elspeth teased. "Won't that be a bit of a strain when you don't believe in Christmas?"

"I can handle it," her brother said.

He could not even make himself sound grouchy. He was so pleased to have the chance to give them the gifts.

"I'm putting up the tree tonight," his mother said. "I could use some help."

Luke pretended he had not heard. It was a fake tree that was sprayed silver. He had disliked it from the minute she brought it home the year before. Elspeth shared his scorn. But both of them ended up helping their mother. And before they went to bed, the first packages were sitting under it.

✶

Then it was Christmas Eve. When Mr. Charles came, Luke was ready and waiting.

"Don't be surprised if we are still at the neighbors' party when you come home," his mother called after him, but he hardly heard her. He had the gifts for Polly and her grandfather hidden inside his jacket.

The gloves fit perfectly.

"Are you sure …?" the old man asked, staring at his gloved hands.

"It was my dad's idea," Luke lied. "He'll be really glad you like them."

He almost gave Polly the cat collar. He was going to put it on her wrist like a bracelet. Then he remembered they were going to church and he waited.

"First we will read the story from the Gospel according to Saint Luke," the minister said.

Luke felt embarrassed but he liked the old words. There were no presents in it though, just the shepherds scared by an angel and then running to see the baby.

They sang about angels. The presents were in the next reading from Matthew's Gospel. Gold and frankincense and myrrh. Not tops or gloves or cat collars. Thinking this, Luke almost laughed aloud.

Even though he still thought he didn't believe, the scripture made the story come alive somehow. No Santa Claus. But a real baby.

When they all joined in to sing "O, come, all ye faithful," Luke felt the song was shouting right at him. Come, come, come, it said. But how could he?

On their way home, he gave Polly the cat collar, sliding it onto her wrist as a shining bracelet. She waved her arm back and forth, beaming as she made the bells tinkle. Clearly, she loved his gift.

Mr. Charles shook his head at Luke.

"You do know she will drive me mad with those," he said.

But Luke could tell he was really pleased. A smile lit up his whole face.

"Jinga-jing, jinga-jing," Polly sang, her funny face shining as brightly as her grandfather's.

Luke helped push the chair back to their door. Then, realizing he had nothing for his sister, he ran to the corner store and bought her a package of gummy bears. It was cheap but she loved gummies. He was cutting through the park when a big car pulled up on the road ahead of him. The passenger door was thrust open and a man's voice, slurred with drink, called out, "Good luck and good riddance, runt."

For one second, Luke thought he was the one being addressed. Then, as the car roared away, he caught sight of the limp bundle lying in the snow. He was staring at it, trying to figure out what it was, when he saw it move. He ran toward it, and got there just as it lifted its head and whimpered. It was a puppy. No, not "it" … she. Luke gathered her up gently and snuggled her small, soft, trembling body against his chest as he looked her over. She was still very young, but her eyes were open wide. One eye had a brown patch over it. Feeling her start to tremble harder, he stopped examining her and tucked her inside the front of his jacket.

"I believe in Christmas," he told her softly. "And you are going to be my present to Jemima and myself. She will love you or else."

The puppy's tail stirred and her quivers eased as she found she was safe and warm. As they neared home, he felt her tongue dart out and lick the tip of his right thumb, which was under her chin. He gasped with delight.

Nobody was in. They had all gone to the neighbors' Christmas Eve party. He breathed a prayer of thanks. He carried the puppy into his bedroom. Then he brought the cat in and introduced her to the pup. He was braced, ready to jump to the defense of whichever animal was getting set upon, but there was no need. The dog was so small that Jemima clearly thought it was up to her to wash her and train her in the way she should go. She flattened the baby out with one motherly paw and began licking her. The puppy's eyes widened but she put up with being scrubbed by the cat's rough tongue. Watching them, Luke smothered his laughter. Then he got busy setting the stage.

He wanted his family all to be surprised at the same moment.

It worked like a charm. He had the two animals cuddled up together in the big wicker clothes basket that had been his grandmother's. He had it placed under the tree where nobody could fail to guess it was a Christmas present. He had tied on a cardboard tag that read, in large black letters, MERRY CHIRSTMAS, JEMIMA—FROM LUKE.

He had no sooner got everything set than he heard them coming. Perfect timing!

Once his mother had had time to calm down, and Elspeth had stopped cooing, and his father had taken enough pictures, his mother asked him what the puppy's name was.

"Merry," Luke said with a grin.

He did not tell them how it was spelled. They did not need to know why he had chosen it. But it was perfect for his pup. Reaching down to pet her, he remembered telling Elspeth that he didn't believe in Christmas. Well, it wasn't true, not any more. He only had to remember Justin spinning his top or Polly ringing her bracelet to know he had changed his mind. He, Luke, was a boy who owned a puppy called Merry and who definitely believed in Christmas, and that was that.

Without Beth

Before the twins were born, their parents had an argument.

"If it's a girl, I want to name her Elizabeth after you," their father said.

"Let's not," their mother said. "Elizabeth the Second! It would sound ridiculous."

When the babies turned out to be twin daughters, their father was inspired. "How about Eliza … and Beth?"

Their mother laughed and gave in.

Beth was the younger by nine minutes but that was the only time she ever let Eliza get ahead of her. Eliza didn't mind. She liked following Beth. Beth made friends for both of them. Beth chose which game they would play. "Hide and Seek," she'd call out.

"Good," Eliza would call back. "You're It."

Beth named their guinea pigs and their dolls. Their favorite dolls were Christmas presents from Great Aunt Emerald the year they were nine. They, too, were identical, but Aunt Emerald had dressed one in red and the other in green.

"How about Holly and Ivy?" Beth asked.

"Perfect," said Eliza. "Mine's Holly."

Beth was the twin most people remembered, even though the girls looked so alike, small for their age, with taffy-colored hair and wide gray-green eyes and one dimple each.

"Eliza, you're just as smart and pretty as your sister," her anxious parents told her.

"I know," said Eliza. "Stop worrying. I could get along fine without Beth if I had to."

As she said the words, a cold finger of fear touched her. Without Beth. She could not bear to think about her life without her twin. But why should she? They had years to go before they would be grown-up and, even then, they could be near each other.

She liked Beth's games and names. She truly wanted to be the lady-in-waiting and the squire and the enemy and, every so often, the loyal hound. She even enjoyed being Beth's stand-in, year after year, in school plays and pageants.

She had all the fun of coming to rehearsals with Mrs. Paganini without ever having to play the parts on stage. She didn't mind being Beth's understudy, but she quaked at the thought of actually speaking lines in front of a live audience.

"It's a good thing I'm healthy, Liza," Beth teased when they were in Grade 7. "Maybe someday I'll get sick, just to see what you'll do."

"Don't," Eliza shivered. "Don't get sick."

The play this year was a comedy about a girl in the olden days, who decided to cook an elaborate New Year's dinner for her large family and assorted guests, and did everything wrong.

Nobody was surprised when Beth was chosen to play the heroine and Mary Lou was given the part of the helpful grandmother. They were by far the best actresses in the class.

Eliza knew all the lines by the second day. She was better at memorizing than her sister. With astonishment, she watched Beth clowning on stage. The play was not all that good. Yet Beth made the mediocre script sparkle. Soon, Eliza was chuckling and, at the sentimental finish, when the girl's granny took a hand and quietly saved the situation, she was blinking back tears.

Someday Beth will be a famous actress, her sister thought.

She was sure Mrs. Paganini agreed with her. The teacher praised everybody, but Beth made her laugh and sometimes even burst into applause.

"This year," the teacher announced, "we're giving two performances. We'll sell tickets and there will be reserved seats. We will donate the money to Famine Relief."

They all practiced harder than ever before. Eliza and Beth were so busy, they almost forgot to buy the family tickets. As it was, they got three in one row and one directly behind.

"I'll sit there," Eliza said.

She was excited about seeing the play from a seat in the audience.

Their mother bought them matching scarlet dresses with lace collars and a little pocket in the skirt. They wore them first to Great Aunt Emerald's Christmas party a few days before the play. Aunt Emerald gave them books, as usual. She also gave Beth a good luck gift to wear on the night of the performance. It was a tiny gold star. Beth laughed and pinned it on.

"Is she really a star?" one of their little cousins asked.

"Don't answer that," Beth said. "It might be unlucky to talk about it ahead of time. You are supposed to say, 'Break a leg.'"

"But stars are lucky," the little boy insisted. "It'll bring good luck to the person who wears it, won't it, Aunt Emerald?"

"That was my intention," his great aunt said with a smile.

But it did not bring good luck to Beth. The next evening, four days before opening night, she got meningitis. It was a word that would make Eliza shiver even when she was an old lady. Beth seemed fine all day, until near suppertime. Then she complained of a bad headache and a stiffness in her neck. Soon she was running a high fever. At nine o'clock, the doctor came and, minutes later, an ambulance was at the door. Beth was driven away with sirens screaming. Her voice, saying goodbye, sounded small and scared.

Mom phoned Aunt Emerald to come and stay with Eliza. She gave her a quick hug. Then she and Dad left for the hospital. Eliza longed to go with them but she didn't ask.

When Aunt Emerald arrived by taxi, Eliza wanted to stay up, but Aunt Emerald fussed over her so much that she finally took refuge in her room. Hers and Beth's.

She got into bed but she could not stay there. She prowled around the room, picking up cassette tapes and books she loved and putting them down again. Even though she did her best to keep her back turned, she kept seeing Beth's empty bed.

Finally, she grew so weary she collapsed on the foot of her own bed and dozed. But, even half-asleep, she knew, deep inside herself, that Beth was leaving her. When her father came, at last, to tell her that her sister had died, Eliza hardly heard his words. She was desperately pushing away the very idea of going on living without Beth.

"I can't do it," she whispered. "I don't know how."

"I know how you feel," said her father. But he could not really know. Beth was not his twin.

Nobody thought of the school play that day, unless it was Mrs. Paganini. She waited a couple of days. Then she came to Eliza's parents. She left it to them to talk with Eliza.

"It is the costume, partly," Eliza's mother said. "It is an old-fashioned Victorian dress, as you know. Beth was smaller than the others. It would fit you, but it can't be made big enough for anyone else. And Mrs. Paganini says that you know all the lines. The part is too long for anyone else to memorize in time. It's up to you, dear. Nobody will blame you if you don't do it. But they have advertised, and opening night is sold out. The money ..."

"I know about the money," Eliza said dully.

She couldn't be Beth. She would make a mess of it. There wasn't even time for her to be in a proper rehearsal. If it weren't for the hungry children, and if it weren't for the other kids, who had been practicing so hard …

It was only when she was getting dressed that Eliza realized that her mother had taken away all of Beth's clothes. Or she thought she had. When Eliza slid the red dress over her head and looked in the mirror, she saw, pinned to the front of it, a small gold star.

As her hand reached up and closed on the tiny brooch, her eyes stung with tears. Then, with trembling fingers, she unfastened it. She was not a star. She knew it, and soon everyone else would know, too.

Yet she did not put the pin in her jewel case or throw it out. She slipped it into the pocket of the dress. There was a chance, a small chance, that it would somehow help her get through.

As the family drove to the school, even Aunt Emerald had nothing much to say. When they got out of the car, Eliza's mother asked if she would like her to help her get her costume on.

Eliza shook her head. She could not trust her voice. She walked around to the dressing room, feeling like a wind-up toy. She answered,

"Hi," whenever anyone said, "Hi, Eliza." Hardly anyone did. When kids saw her coming, most of them looked away.

Eliza slid the frumpy gingham dress that was her costume on over Beth's dress. Then she put on the pioneer girl's apron and tied it in a bow behind her back. When she was done, she patted her front, feeling the tiny star where it lay hidden beneath the costume, in the pocket of the red dress.

"Are you ready, dear?" Mrs. Paganini asked from outside the door.

"Coming," she answered in a voice that shook. She wondered what would happen if she threw up on stage.

Mrs. Paganini took Eliza's cold hand and squeezed it.

"This way, darling," she said, looking as though she were about to break down.

Eliza took a deep breath and followed her. When they were on the stage, she walked over to the curtains and parted them slightly. Behind her, Mrs. Paganini blew her nose. But Eliza did not hear. She was staring through the narrow slit at the rows of people. There were her parents and Great Aunt Emerald. And, in Eliza's empty seat, just behind them, sat her sister Beth.

"It isn't," Eliza breathed and rubbed her eyes.

Beth was still there. She had on a scarlet dress. Her eyes were smiling straight at her sister. And, as Eliza stared, she gave the little salute that, between the two of them, had always meant, whatever happened, they were a team.

"Mrs. Paganini," Eliza said hoarsely. "Come and look at the people."

"I know, I know," the teacher said. "It's a full house."

She took Eliza's place, peered out at the audience, and smiled broadly.

"They're all rooting for you, sweetheart," she said, turning to pat Eliza's arm. Then she headed for the wings, calling over her shoulder, "Break a leg, honey. Curtain in two minutes."

Eliza laughed softly. She did not look to see if Beth was still there. She moved to the table and took her place, pulling the thick cookbook toward her. She pushed back her hair as the curtains parted and blew out a loud, thoroughly exasperated sigh.

Before she had said a word, the surprised audience had laughed.

Her family must be astonished, she thought, as she opened her mouth to speak the first line. Then she pushed away the thought and became the girl in the play. Even though everybody in the auditorium knew about Beth's death, Eliza soon made them forget and keep chuckling. She played the part almost as Beth would have done. But several times she did something Beth had never thought of doing. Whenever she did, laughter rang out. Until the final moment. Then, when she and Mary Lou hugged each other, they had the audience in tears.

When the cast went forward for curtain calls, Eliza was given a standing ovation. Smiling and bowing, she knew that she had earned it. Not Beth this time. But Eliza on her own.

And Beth had been there.

The curtains closed and the excited players began to troop off stage to get changed. Mary Lou lingered to speak to the teacher. Hoping to escape without having to talk to the others, Eliza stood still, waiting for the way to clear.

Then Mrs. Paganini's excited voice broke through to her.

"Girls, did you realize that there was only one empty seat in the auditorium," she said. "To tell you the truth, I thought, at first, we would have to cancel the performance, Eliza. I'd never seen you act without Beth, so I wasn't sure. But you were wonderful, you and Mary Lou both."

As the teacher turned to smile at Mary Lou, Eliza wanted to tell her that she had not been without Beth. But nobody would understand.

When she had taken off her costume, Eliza reached into the pocket of the red dress and fished out the tiny gold star. She held it in her cupped palm, remembering the moment when she had seen Beth. Then, before anyone could interrupt her, she pinned the star onto the spot where her twin had fastened it the night of Aunt Emerald's party.

"We're still a team," she whispered. Then she went to find her family.

Patrick's Tree

Christmas was still thirteen days away when Patrick Fisher first saw the tree. He stopped dead in his tracks to stare at it. It stood in the tall bay window in the stone house two blocks from the Fishers' cottage. Gran and he called the stone house "The Mansion," because it looked so stately and important, like a house in an old-fashioned book.

Patrick had never seen anything as magnificent as the tree. It stood straight, filling the tall window from top to bottom. Dozens of colored lights were strung through its dark branches. It was also festooned with glass balls, small carvings of animals, and expertly made origami creatures.

Patrick had folded paper cranes himself, but here were frogs and rabbits and birds of all kinds.

"Awesome," he whispered.

He took a step closer and strained to catch a glimpse of other treasures half-hidden in the evergreen boughs. There were a couple of homemade dough angels, a small plush elephant, and a string of bells.

Someone had hung bright strands of tinsel so that each thread dangled separately. Seeing them gleaming against the dark needles, Patrick knew why he had been told to stop tossing tinsel at the tree in wads when he was a little boy. Teasing the thin ribbons apart must take ages, though.

Suddenly he jumped backwards, almost toppling over. He had been so intent on seeing every ornament that he had not noticed someone arriving on the other side of the glass. A man had moved a stepladder into place. He was concentrating on making sure it was steady and had no attention to spare for the world beyond the window. At last, he climbed up and carefully fixed an angel to the topmost twig. He placed her so that one of the white bulbs fitted inside her.

He climbed down and went across the room. He must have turned on a switch because then, all the lights glowed, and the angel shone with a special radiance. She had her arms stretched out and her feathery wings spread wide. Patrick felt as though she was shining just for him.

Then he snapped out of his trance and realized how dark the sky had become. Gran would be home long ago and wondering where he was. He tore his gaze from the splendor in the window and headed for home at a run.

"Good timing," Gran said as he burst in. "Take off your coat and come to the table before your supper gets cold."

While he was eating his shepherd's pie, Patrick began describing the marvelous Christmas tree in the Mansion's front window. As he pictured for her each of the precious ornaments, his grandmother sighed. Then she broke in on his torrent of talk.

"Patrick, you must know we haven't enough room here for a tree like that. We couldn't afford it, either. Those big trees are expensive."

Patrick stared at her. He had never imagined for one moment that they could have such a prize. Why couldn't she just listen? Anger bubbled up in him and he began to shove his chair back. But she held onto him.

"We have the table tree though, Patrick. I know it's not the same, but you've always liked it," she said.

Patrick remembered the table tree, of course. Mama and he had moved in with his grandparents just before Christmas when he was almost four. Mama had been all excited when she had found the table tree at a sale and bought it for Gran.

It was a ceramic tree. It had a light inside it and stood about a foot high. It was green and cone-shaped, and had small holes all over it into which you fitted tiny bulbs of many colors. Then you switched on the light and the table tree was transformed.

Every year since, Patrick and his grandparents had joined in, choosing which tiny colored bulb would go into which small hole.

They had loved doing it, taking their time, consulting each other about the rightness of each decision, not switching the light on until every bulb was in its place.

The first year, when Mama had been there, too, she had tried to rush them.

"What does it matter where they go? At this rate, we'll be here all night," she had snapped.

"We are enjoying ourselves, Jeanette," Gran had told her daughter firmly. "You go along and do whatever it is you are wanting to do and leave us be."

Mama had been mad, but a look from Grandpa had stopped her fussing. Patrick had been relieved when she had taken her cell phone into the bedroom and left them to their fun. That spring, she had gone off with a man named Max, who had promised to get her a job as a model.

"I'll come back for you, baby," she had called to her son before Max's car pulled away. "I promise."

But she had not come. She had phoned a few times, mailed him postcards, and sent presents twice. When he was five, she got him three yellow duckies to play with in his bath, and when he was eight, she sent a sailor suit meant for a much smaller boy.

"I wish I knew her address so I could send her a picture of you," Gran had said, holding up the little sailor outfit. "You would have looked adorable in this a few years ago."

DO NOT OPEN UNTIL CHRISTMAS

Patrick still liked the rubber duckies.

The Christmas after Mama left, Grandpa had begun playing The Table Tree Game in earnest, claiming that certain bulbs could not bear being close to others. The game, which Grandpa made funnier and more complicated every year, had been one of the neat things about Christmas. His laugh booming out had been far better than Santa's "Ho, ho, ho!"

But Patrick had not heard that laugh since Grandpa had had his stroke. The man lying in the hospital bed never laughed. This year, they would have to get through Christmas without him.

Patrick blinked away tears and rocked his chair onto its back legs. He grabbed a spoon and started drumming on the table with it. Tappity-bang! Tappity-BANG!

"Is there any dessert?" he yelled over the racket.

"Stop that, Patrick. I got ice cream," his grandmother said. "That special kind with candy canes in it. You fetch it and I'll get the bowls. I took some over to your grandpa this afternoon."

Patrick dropped the spoon and ran to the freezer compartment in the fridge. He was pleased to see that she had bought the medium-sized container, not the small one. He spooned a large bite into his waiting mouth and felt better as its cold sweetness slid down his throat. Then he shot a sidewise look at Gran. Was she angry?

"I'll get the tree out as soon as we've finished," she said quietly. But her eyes were anxious and he could see her hand shake.

"Great," he said, trying to appear thrilled. "That'll be fine."

They unpacked the box together. The table tree, freed of its wrappings, was just as Patrick had remembered. Only smaller and dimmer. He did his best to act excited as he put in half-a-dozen of the little lights, but his heart wasn't in it. Gran knew, of course. When his fingers slowed, she moved the box out of his reach.

"Leave it for now. We can finish it after you do your homework," she said. "Then, when we go to see Grandpa, we can tell him we have it all set up."

Patrick felt a lump as big as an apple squeeze inside his throat. He dashed into the bathroom and slammed the door. The crash was comforting. He flushed the toilet, filled the basin, and splashed the water as though he were scrubbing his hands and his face. Then he squared his shoulders and came back out.

He crossed the room without looking at the table tree and got his homework. He did the math questions quickly, not bothering to check his work. Who cared if his answers were wrong? Not Patrick Fisher.

As he jammed the books into his backpack again, he glanced over at Gran. She gave him a sheepish look. She had put almost all the bulbs in without his help.

"I meant to wait for us to do them together," she said, "but once you start, it's like eating peanuts. Come and do the last three."

He did not want to, but he went and put in one red, one blue, and a green. They looked okay. Then Gran pressed the switch and the light inside shone out, transforming the small, insignificant tree into a thing of enchantment.

In that moment, Patrick saw the anxiety in Gran's eyes give way to wonder. And he felt the same delight.

"That's awesome," he said, forgetting he had said it about the other tree.

After she read him the next chapter of *Angel Square*, he went to brush his teeth. Standing in front of the bathroom mirror, he thought about the two trees, the tall one in the bay window and the small one on the table. For that one moment, when the light came on, it had seemed magical. But now it was ordinary again. Not like a real tree at all.

When Gran came to his room to say goodnight, she paused by his bed and said, "I'm sorry we can't have a real tree, Patrick."

"It's okay," he mumbled. "'Night."

In the dark kitchen, the table tree glowed. Gran stood and looked down at it. In the five years since Jeanette had left her little boy with them, her husband had made the little tree so special. But now Andrew was in the hospital, one side paralyzed from a stroke. When she and Patrick visited him, the boy and his grandfather smiled politely at each other, but Andrew could not speak clearly and, when he could not find the word he wanted, he flushed and shut his lips. His speech therapist told them they must encourage him but, no matter what they did, he refused to try again. Then she would see the fear looking out of her grandson's eyes and she knew Andrew must see it, too.

"If you have any magic left," Pat's grandmother murmured to the tree, "send my boys a happy Christmas."

✳

Every day that week, Patrick stopped on his way home to gaze at the tall tree in the window. He never saw anybody gathered around it after that first time, but often another decoration or two had been added.

The tree would not have fit into their little house, but he wished he could take one just like it to set up in Grandpa's room at the hospital. It was such a sad room, with its dull green walls and a small window through which the sun never shone. There were no proper pictures hung up, just calendars.

He swung away and started for home.

As he loped up the short walk to his own front door, he heard laughter. He knew that voice. At one and the same moment, his heart leaped up and his stomach clenched.

"Mama," he whispered.

Had she come for him? Glimpsing her through the window as she leaned to move one of the tiny bulbs on the table tree, he was sure she had not. But she was as pretty as the angel on the Mansion's treetop. Seeing her, his breath quickened with excitement.

He ran up the steps and thrust open the door. Both women turned. Grandma was beaming.

"Look who's here, Patrick," she cried.

Then his mother swooped upon him and gathered him into a smothering hug. His face was squashed against her front.

"How dare you grow so big!" she said into his ear. "My baby, do you remember your old mother?"

He pulled away. She wanted him to say she was not old, he knew, but he did not. What a dumb question! Of course he remembered her.

"Sure, Mama," he said. "You still smell just the same."

She clapped her hands and gave a trill of laughter.

"Of course I do, sweetie," she said. "I have worn the same perfume since I was sixteen. Mother, he's adorable!"

Why, why was she gushing like this? Babies were adorable, but he was not a baby any longer.

Gran sent him a look of sympathy, told him to hang up his coat, and went to get the supper ready to serve.

"It is so nice that you came today, Jeanette," she said, as she set down the dishes. "Patrick and I take your father his supper on Tuesday right after we've had ours. He'll be thrilled to see you."

Mama gave a little snort and plunked herself down on the chair facing the food.

"I'll just bet," she said, her sweet voice roughening. "He wasn't so fond of me last time I saw him."

"Don't speak of him that way," Gran said.

"No, don't," Patrick muttered, glaring at his mother.

"Sorry," she said. But her eyes were still stormy.

Gran patted her hand.

"He was worried about you," she said. "We must hurry or he'll think we aren't coming."

As the three of them got into Mama's rented car, Patrick knew this was his chance to show them the tree. He persuaded his mother to go past the stone house.

"Gran, look," he said, pointing.

His grandmother gasped.

"Oh, Patrick, how beautiful! I see why you love it," she said.

He waited for his mother to agree.

"Well, those people certainly have more money than sense," she said at last. "That thing must cost a ruddy fortune."

Patrick shifted his weight so that his body was further away from hers. Grandpa would love the tree, he was certain. He wished he had not talked Mama into looking. He ought to have known how it would be.

When Grandpa saw her, he went utterly still.

"Oh, you poor old thing!" she exclaimed much too loudly. Then she leaned over and gave him a noisy kiss. He flinched. Her lipstick left a scarlet smear on his cheek.

"Jeanette has come for a visit," Gran told him. "Patrick and I got quite a surprise, didn't we, son?"

DO NOT OPEN UNTIL CHRISTMAS

"Yeah," Patrick said.

Grandpa closed his eyes. Patrick saw his hands were trembling and pulled the blanket up to cover them. Then he moved between his mother and the bed. She was starting to blubber.

"Quit bawling," he whispered.

Gran swung the bed table across and got ready to give her husband his supper. Grandpa still lay with his eyes closed. His face looked pale as wax and very old. Patrick could not understand it. Six months ago, Grandpa had been full of life, a different person. Where had that man gone?

"Take your mother down to the cafeteria for a cup of coffee," his grandmother told him. "She's tired out from her trip."

As they walked down the hall, Mama began to cry harder. She moaned so that passing people stared. Her son longed to slap her. Instead he blurted out the question he knew would distract her, the one he had wanted to put to her ever since he had heard her laughing.

"Did you come to get me?"

"What?" she said, as though she had not heard him.

"You promised you would come back for me," he half-shouted. "Is that why you came?"

Whatever she said, he knew he would not go. He remembered what it was like living with her. But she should admit she had broken her promise.

She began to talk fast, telling him all her terrible problems and reminding him that she had Max to think about, not just herself. Max had had to come up to Hamilton to collect some money a guy owed him, and so she had taken the chance to come along and visit.

"I just had to see you," she said in a sort of whimper. "After all, you're my baby."

Patrick led her into the cafeteria. She jabbered on, all through drinking two cups of coffee and eating a ham and cheese sandwich. Finally, he broke in.

"It's okay, Mama," he told her, keeping his voice low, wishing he had not asked. "I'm happy here. Stop fussing."

"You sound just like Dad," she said.

"Thanks," her son said. "Let's go."

The next day, when he reached the big house, it was clear that the people inside were giving a party. Cars were pulling up and people's voices were calling out holiday greetings. But Patrick did not stop. He had his own party planned. When he reached home, he knew before he got the door fully open that his mother had gone. When Gran put out her arms to hug him, he smiled and fended her off.

"Don't get your tights in a tangle, Grandma," he said, imitating his grandfather's way of teasing her. "I knew she'd take off. She told me Max might be picking her up."

Without taking his coat off, he headed for the Table Tree and began removing the small bulbs and putting them in their box.

"Patrick, what are you doing?" his grandmother asked.

As he handed her the box of bulbs, he realized he felt years older than he had before Mama had come. He laughed and saw the anxiety begin to leave Gran's eyes.

"We're taking Christmas to Grandpa," he told her. "You hold onto these. I'll carry the tree. Come on. Let's get moving."

"Oh, Patrick," his grandmother breathed, hurrying to get her coat on.

When they came into his dark room, Grandpa seemed to be asleep. Grandma put out her hand to turn on the light but Patrick stopped her. He put the tree on the bedside table and pointed to the electric outlet. She nodded and plugged the tree in.

Working fast in the dim light coming through the open door, Patrick popped the bulbs into their holes. When the Table Tree was ready, he nodded to his grandmother. He was positive Grandpa was not really sleeping.

"Open your eyes, Grandpa," he said.

As his grandfather looked at him, Gran pressed the switch and the Table Tree's lights flashed on. They seemed to glow with an extra brightness as though they knew it mattered.

As the old man stared at the little tree, Gran pushed the button that raised the head of his bed. When Patrick took his hand, he held on as though the boy's fingers were a rope thrown to rescue him.

"Oh, boy," he said. "Oh, oh, boy."

Patrick tried to say, "Merry Christmas, Grandpa," but his throat had closed, so he put his free arm around his grandfather's shoulders and hugged him.

Gran said it for both of them. "Merry Christmas, Andrew."

Grandpa pointed at the red bulb near the top.

"No," he managed. "No."

"You think it needs a green one," Patrick said. He moved to the bedside table and reached to swap the little lights.

"Ya," Andrew Fisher said. "Good, good!"

Then he laughed. Hearing the sound he had so missed, Patrick felt like bursting into song.

He turned to look at the little tree instead. Although it had no fancy decorations and no angel on the top, it went on steadily shining.

Patrick reached out one finger to touch the topmost bulb.

"Way to go, little tree," he whispered.

Gabriel's Angels

When Gabriel was little and her world was a happy place, she loved listening to Mom's stories about her own personal guardian angel, who came to her rescue when she was in a fix.

"I can't just call on her without doing my best to work it out," she said. "But when I can't manage, I whisper, 'Please, help me.' And then, I find what I've lost, or I remember what I've forgotten. It's miraculous."

"Does she always come?" Gabriel had asked.

She could tell that this question made her mother uncomfortable, but she wanted an answer. Her mother would chuckle and stroke her daughter's glossy black curls.

"It's hard to know for sure, since angels are invisible," she would say. "Someday, you will find out but, right now, you are my angel."

Gabriel wished she would be serious. How could there be so

many pictures of angels if they were invisible? How did artists show them dressed in white and having wings? They also had halos sometimes and always golden hair, especially the little baby ones.

Mom had named her Gabriel after an angel, but she did not look one bit like the ones on Christmas cards. She looked like her father, dark-skinned with black hair and deep brown eyes. She had never asked her mother outright if there were brown-skinned angels, but she was pretty sure there were not.

When she was small, they had gone to church once, and she had seen two tall angels in a stained-glass window. They had been magnificent winged beings, towering above the people in the pews. They had been holding trumpets, she thought. Gabriel had been scared that they might climb out of the colored window and come swooping down to grab her. She had started to cry and they had taken her out, but she had never told them what had frightened her.

Then, when she was seven, Dad had lost his job and her brother Michael was born. Everything changed after that. Even though Mom named him after an archangel, Michael was not an ordinary baby. He was stiff to hold, and his eyes sometimes swung around in off-beat directions. His right arm waved about, too, in a strange way, and the left one just hung down limply, like a rag doll's.

"Maybe he'll conduct symphonies," Dad growled once.

Gabriel had been mad at him for saying that. Michael could not wave his arm on purpose, like the orchestra conductor she had seen on TV. Her little brother's one arm jerked about and hit things off the table sometimes. Dad must know he couldn't control it.

She wanted to say so but she bit back the words. Her father hated them talking about Michael's problems. He believed the little boy did not understand anything they said, but Gabriel knew he was wrong. As Michael grew from a baby into a toddler, he took it all in. His sister could see laughter and sometimes hurt in his eyes. He always pulled himself across the floor to lean against her after Dad had gone. Then Gabriel would hug him, and he would give his crooked smile back.

Soon it was clear that Michael did not learn the things other babies did. He could not stay balanced when Mom tried to sit him up. He made sounds, but none of them were attempts at words. He made noises and pointed to things he wanted, but he was three before Gabriel heard him starting to speak. Her parents did not believe her when she told them he was calling her "Ga," and saying "Mom-mom" for Mom.

"I think you are dreaming," her mother said when Gabriel had tried to make her listen.

Dad had said he would have to go to some special school, but neither of Michael's parents seemed to know how to find help for him.

At last, they took him to the doctor, who told them he had cerebral palsy. Afterwards, she sent somebody she called a therapist to work with him.

Gabriel loved Mrs. Lighthart. She was patient, quick to laugh, always turning things into games, and she really enjoyed Michael.

"You can help him more than anyone, Gabriel," she told his sister quietly. "Play with him and talk to him. Make him take turns. Roll a ball back and forth. He understands more than your parents believe."

Gabriel had tried to get her mother to listen to the therapist but, when she came, Mom only wanted to talk about herself. Mrs. Lighthart listened to her pour out her troubles and, later on, went back to explaining things to Michael's sister.

Gabriel tried to do what she suggested. But Dad got fed up with the program.

"For God's sake, Leda, face facts," he snarled at Mom. "The boy's the way he is, and nothing can be done about it."

And one day, when Mrs. Lighthart arrived, he told her they didn't want her coming any longer.

Mrs. Lighthart protested but Dad started to yell, "We know what's best for our own kid. When we need the Ministry poking its nose in, we'll call you."

And Mrs. Lighthart had not come back.

Gabriel kept helping her brother to play with the things the woman had left: a mirror, a squeezy ball, some special blocks, and a hand puppet. But she made sure they were put out of sight before her father came in. Michael always got excited when his sister took the things out.

"There's nothing wrong with us a family camping trip won't fix," Dad announced the summer after Mrs. Lighthart stopped coming.

But a heat wave and swarms of black flies turned the trip into a nightmare. When Michael's black fly and mosquito bites made him cry until he choked, Dad swore at him and packed everything up again. They left for home an hour later.

"I should have known," Gabriel's father grumbled, glaring at his son who, by then, was running a fever.

Then Dad was fired again, and Gabriel's family began coming apart. The noise of their parents quarreling kept both children awake into the night. Then their mother would begin to nag about needing money.

There was no more talk of angels. There was only mounting anger and constant worry.

Gabriel tried to get her mother to ask her guardian angel for help. But Mom just shook her head.

Finally the long hot summer ended and school opened. Gabriel loved school. When she got home and they were alone, she taught Michael. Now that she was ten and her brother was four, he loved to hear her read aloud the primary books she checked out of the library. As she read them over and over, she could tell he was not just looking at the pictures but following the words.

"Why are you bringing home baby books?" Dad demanded one night.

"Leave her be. Her teacher told me she's practically a genius," Mom said wearily. "Why aren't you reading the Help Wanted ads?"

When she said it once too often, he walked out, slamming the door behind him so hard the glass pane in it cracked across. Gabriel stared at it and waited for Mom to react, but she just sighed. When a week went by and he had not returned, Gabriel asked her mother if she had heard from him.

Her mother pretended she had not heard. Half an hour later, she had gone to bed, leaving Gabriel to find something for them to eat. She made up a package of macaroni that they downed without looking at each other. Then she put a plate of it on the bedside table for her mother and went to do her homework.

✶

"Are you Gabriel Thomas?" the new principal asked her one morning.

Gabriel nodded, hoping against hope that he wasn't going to ask her to get her mother to come in for a teacher-parent visit.

"My wife said I should tell you 'Hi' from her. Do you remember Mrs. Lighthart?" he asked, smiling at her.

Gabriel stared at the man. Then she smiled back. Why had she not connected their names? She wanted to send back a message to Mrs. Lighthart, but she did not know where to begin.

"Of course I do," she said.

The man laughed.

"I'll tell her about that smile," he said.

As time passed, the children's clothes grew too small and they had holes in their shoes. Gabriel had no warm coat and ended up wearing an old windbreaker that had been Mom's. It was too big and not warm, but it was better than nothing.

There soon was not enough money to buy good food. They began eating mostly cold cereal or bread and peanut butter.

They moved in with Mom's cousin Lucianne for "a few days." Lucianne was a neat, fussy lady who was not at ease with her cousin's children. She never looked directly at Michael and seldom spoke to either of them.

At first, Mom told her that Dad would soon be back. But as time passed, she stopped mentioning him.

"You'll have to put the boy away somewhere, Leda," Lucianne kept telling Mom. Gabriel hated this. She made Michael sound like groceries or laundry, not a person. She wanted to shout at her to stop, but she bit back the words, knowing her mother needed the woman's support. At last, Lucianne told them they would have to go.

"Lu, we can't …" Mom began.

"You'll have to manage, Leda. I told you not to marry him," Lucianne said and left.

"Gabriel, are things all right at home?" Mr. Lighthart asked her when they met in the hall.

She longed to tell the man everything, but there were kids and teachers all around. Maybe they weren't listening, but she could not risk it. She remembered Dad's fury when the woman next door had given her a sweater because she had no warm coat. "Charity" he called it—and told her to give the sweater back. Mom had taken it from her without a word, and Gabriel had never seen it again.

"Why is he like that?" she had asked when her father was out.

"He can't bear to be pitied," Mom had said.

Gabriel had not understood what was so terrible about pity. But now she forced a smile and managed to tell Mr. Lighthart everything was fine. Then she pushed her way out of the school.

"Wanna come to my house and play Barbies?" Mandy asked as they crossed the snowy playground.

"Can't," Gabriel growled, without looking around. "I'm not allowed."

She did not tell the girl that she had no Barbies, or any other toys like the ones Mandy and her friends played with. The only game she and Michael had was an old Chinese checker board that had been Mom's. They played it by her pointing to each marble and her brother sort of nodding. Watching them drove their mother crazy.

"How do you know what he wants you to do?" she asked.

Gabriel did not try to explain. Playing their way took endless patience, and her mother was not a patient person.

She did wish the TV would stop endlessly showing the newest toys. Christmas was the day rich kids got presents, and poor kids like the two of them got Salvation Army baskets of food. Last year, because they had moved just before Christmas, even the basket had failed to arrive.

Trying to get away from her thoughts, Gabriel broke into a run. Maybe Mom would have gone to the Food Bank and they would have something filling for supper. All they had left to live on now was the welfare check, and it seemed to disappear in no time flat.

"I'll get work soon," Mom promised in a hopeless voice.

By now, Gabriel knew this wouldn't happen. Who would hire her mother, looking the way she did?

"Call your angel," she suggested, trying to make her mother smile.

Her mother did not answer. She just slumped down on the bed and went back to watching *American Idol*.

Gabriel now knew the truth about her mother's precious angel, though. She had come back from the bathroom a week ago and caught her mother hunting for something. She was in a frenzy. Gabriel opened her mouth to ask her what the matter was, when her mother suddenly folded her hands, stared up at the light fixture, and said, "I've done all I can. Help me, angel. Help me!" Then she closed her eyes and stretched out her hands, and brought one of them down on a magazine that slid away, revealing the scissors.

"Oh, thank you!" Mom sang out, clutching them to her chest. "You did it again."

Then she saw Gabriel watching.

"Gabriel, did you see? My angel found the scissors," she told her daughter, her eyes actually shining.

She went babbling on, but Gabriel was sure she had simply remembered where she herself had put them down. Maybe talking to "the angel" cleared her muddled thinking. But whatever she claimed, the scissors had not really been lost, and it was not an angel who located them but her mother's own right hand.

So, no angel would save them when they called.

At least they still had the television and the phone. Then these were gone, too, and the landlord told them he was evicting them because the rent had not been paid.

Mom finally called the Welfare Office.

The welfare lady, Ms. Smith-Walter, who had told her mother she must go to a lecture on how to budget, found them a basement room they could move into. It was equipped with a hot plate in a closet. They had to share a bathroom with the family next door, who could not speak English. It was downtown and the noise never let up. But they could just manage to pay the rent.

"Now, try to plan and make the money stretch a bit better," the woman said as she left, avoiding looking into their tired faces.

"She's so mean," Gabriel burst out.

"I think she just hates her job. She's sick of talking to poor people," Mom said, collapsing onto the bed with a groan.

The lady from the other apartment burst in at the door. She took

DO NOT OPEN UNTIL CHRISTMAS

one look and ran out again, but she came right back with a pot of thick soup and some homemade bread. Gabriel, who had wondered what they would have for supper, thought maybe the neighbor was an angel. Michael waved at her and beamed, and she leaned down to stroke his grimy cheek.

A month later, when they ran out of food, her mother brought a man home. He was a big man called Joe. He gave Gabriel's mother some money to buy food but, when she asked for more, in a small, begging voice that made Gabriel squirm with shame, the guy left, banging the door behind him just as Dad had done.

He came back after the children were in bed in the curtained-off corner where they slept. Michael had fallen asleep but Gabriel lay awake, listening. They were drinking, she could tell, as the man's voice got louder and started to slur. Then she heard her mother cry out and they seemed to be fighting. Gabriel stayed very still, wishing she had an angel who would come. When he was gone at last, and she went to see how her mother was, she found she had a split lip and a bruise that would turn into a black eye. She was weeping hopelessly and, when Gabriel tried to get her to talk, she realized that her mother had been drinking, too. When she tried to talk, she was not making sense.

Gabriel locked the door and then began to try to get her mother to go to bed. It was more than she could manage. Finally, she got her onto the bed and covered her with a blanket, and went back to her own cot.

A couple of hours later, Joe came back and hammered on the door, but Gabriel made no move to let him in. Finally, she heard a police car drive up and he was taken away.

Then it was nearly Christmas.

"Gabriel Thomas," Mr. Lighthart called, as Gabriel started for home on the last day of school before the Christmas vacation. "My wife asked me to give you this."

Gabriel took the envelope he was holding out to her. She ducked her head so she would not have to meet his eyes. She could not bear to open it there. She shoved it into the pocket of the jacket she was wearing.

"Tell her, thanks," she got out, turning away.

"And Merry Christmas, Gabriel," the man called after her. "This must be a special holiday for you, since you're named after an angel."

"Yeah," Gabriel muttered and ran.

But when she got home, it felt not one bit like Christmas.

"We'll have to go to the Food Bank again," she told her mother after inspecting the empty shelves.

"It isn't open until next week," Mom said dully, sinking down on the edge of the sagging bed.

Her voice sounded flattened, as though Joe had not only punched her face but knocked all the stuffing out of her.

Michael must have felt as frightened as his big sister did, because he gave one of his strange up-and-down howls. Used as she was to the sound, the sadness in it made Gabriel shudder. She waited for their mother to order him to shut up, but she did not even glance at the distressed little boy. She just sat, slumped over, reminding Gabriel of a beached whale she had seen once on TV.

"The creature is still alive but she is doomed," the commentator had said.

Her mother couldn't be doomed. She was staring into space as though her children were not present, did not even exist. Michael crawled over to his sister and held onto her foot. He was whimpering softly.

"Did you feed him?" Gabriel shouted at her mother. Sometimes, having to do something for Michael would pull her back to herself.

"We've run out of his food," she whispered, without opening her eyes.

"Give me money. I'll go get some," Gabriel snapped at her. Trying hard to sound adult and powerful, she held out her hand.

Mom made no move. Her eyes did not even blink. Her handbag was under the coffee table. Gabriel pulled it out and looked in the limp change purse, even though she could tell, from the moment she picked it up, that there was not so much as a nickel inside it. She dropped it and searched the rest of the bag. There were some used tissues, a package of lifesavers with three left in it, a lipstick, other bits of make-up, garbage ...

She handed her brother the lifesavers and was rewarded with one of his rare, crooked smiles, as he began to pull the paper off.

Gabriel turned back to their mother. She had not stirred.

Gabriel waited for a response. When none came, she grabbed hold of the woman's limp shoulders and shook her as hard as she could. Without speaking or opening her eyes, Mom slid out of Gabriel's grip and lay sprawled on the bed. Gabriel felt fear course through her. Was her mother unconscious? What should she do?

There was nothing she could do. Even the neighbor who had brought them soup the day they moved in had gone away. No matter how hard she wracked her brain, Gabriel could not come up with anything she could do to rescue them.

Michael, unable to get the paper off the lifesavers, was eating them now, paper and all. But three candies would not be enough for him.

"Oh, Michael, I don't know what to do," she wailed.

He reached out and patted her foot, doing his level best to make her smile.

As she stretched out her arms to give him a hug, something fell out of her pocket. She stared at it. Then she remembered. Mr. Lighthart had given it to her.

For a long minute, she let it lie where it had fallen. What use could it be to her at this moment?

Then Michael reached over and shoved it toward her, his eyes bright with curiosity.

Gabriel picked it up and slowly ripped it open. A Christmas

card fell out. She almost threw it back down on the floor when she saw the picture on the front.

It was an angel. It wasn't a silly little cherub, either. It was a tall man with a trumpet in his hands. And he seemed to be staring right at her.

She put it down long enough to take off her jacket and scarf. The jacket was an old windbreaker that had been Mom's when she was younger. That was why the pocket had been large enough to hold the card.

"Ope," Michael said. "Ope."

"I will," she said, her voice sharp. Why couldn't he leave her be? Once she opened the card, she would know it would be of no help. If she didn't hurry, she could hope a little longer.

But she opened it at last. There was a poem in it and, under the poem, Mrs. Lighthart had written something.

She forced herself to read the poem first. It was a verse from one of the carols they had sung at school.

Oh, holy child of Bethlehem, it began,

Descend to us, we pray.

But those weren't the words that leapt out at her. They came further down.

We hear the Christmas angels

Their great glad tidings tell …

Her eyes dropped to the message Michael's therapist had written.

Dear Gabriel, I hope you and Michael are okay. My husband thinks you might be needing some help. I am enclosing my address and phone number, in case. Please don't hesitate to call me. If you need help, come anytime.

With love, Angie Lighthart

The address was on Clover Street. Gabriel knew where that was. It was a long way away but she was sure she could find it.

She read the words aloud to her little brother. He patted her foot again and nodded his head.

"Okay," she said, her voice trembling. "I'll try to find them. You stay with Mom until I get back."

Michael laughed. She knew it was funny. He couldn't leave their mother. But it seemed right to put him in charge.

"I'll be back as soon as I can," she promised and pulled the jacket back on. As she reached the door, she looked back. Michael was waving at her. She knew, suddenly, that he believed she would make it. He trusted her. She waved back, opened the door, and set out.

She ran the first couple of blocks and then slowed down. It was bitterly cold and she was soon shivering. When her teeth began to chatter, she looked for some sort of shelter. Just ahead of her was a church. She was about to pound on the big door when someone opened it, as though they knew she was wanting in. She ducked into the entry and heard singing. They were having a Christmas Eve service. It was beautifully warm. Whoever had opened the door had

DO NOT OPEN UNTIL CHRISTMAS

gone. The rest of them were all inside. Hugging her still shivering self, she followed the music. They were singing the words on the card.

"We hear the Christmas angels

The great glad tidings tell …"

The moment she heard them mention angels, she knew she must set out again, however cold it was.

She ran out the door. Her face was stinging and her feet felt like blocks of ice, but she did not let herself stop again. After what seemed like years, she was sure she must be near the place. Clover. There it was.

She looked up the short street, bright with Christmas lights. Only one house was dark. She plodded toward it, her heart heavy with the conviction that it would be the one she had come to find.

It was. She took out the card once more to make sure, and saw the names written out in full.

Angela and Mike Lighthart.

Angel names. What had Mom said? You have to call to your angel. Whisper. That was it.

"Please," Gabriel whispered into the night. "Please."

Then she heard the car coming and turned. They were speeding toward her on "bended wing."

"Gabriel!" Mrs. Lighthart's voice called. Gabriel wanted to run to her, but she could not seem to move. She watched the car doors open and the passengers scramble out.

Then Mrs. Lighthart was reaching for her. As the woman's arms enfolded her, Gabriel realized Mom had been right all along. She was wrong about them being invisible, but she was right about them coming to your rescue when you needed them.

Mrs. Lighthart would set things straight.

"Let me, Angie," her husband said. And he picked Gabriel up as though she were Michael's size. Then he carried her out of the cold night in which she had been lost for so long into the sanctuary of his home. As he set her down on the couch and tucked a warm blanket around her, his wife set a match to the fire. Then Gabriel heard her murmur, "Mike, go get her mother and Michael. We can put them up here until we work things out."

Knowing she and her family were safe, Gabriel was letting herself sink into sleep, when she heard the church bells start to ring. Christmas morning had come.

The Different Doll

Flora May Kerr knew she was supposed to be having a wonderful time, but she wished she could go home instead. Aunt May, who was really not their aunt but their mother's best friend, had taken her and her older brother Robert to the Santa Claus Parade and, when it was done, the three of them were going to Eaton's Toyland to choose the presents she would give them for Christmas. They had done the same thing for four years and, until today, Flora had enjoyed herself.

But today it was snowing and cold, and she was fed up.

First, Dad had driven them to the station to catch the train that morning. She had quite liked that part. Then they had ridden on a streetcar to a corner where they could watch the Santa Claus Parade go by. They found a place to stand where Aunt May was sure they would be able to see everything. But, while they waited, the wind sharpened and it began to snow. Soon Flora's glasses got covered with wet flakes that she had to keep wiping off. While they stood and stood, her toes, in the new boots Mom had bought her, grew chilled and then frozen into lumps of ice. That was how they felt, anyway. She tried stamping but it did not help.

Robert looked at her when she whimpered softly and asked if she was okay. If Aunt May had not turned to listen to her answer, she would have told him about her frozen toes, but what could he do?

"I'm fine," she said, trying not to cry.

Robert patted her on the back.

"You'll feel better when you see the clowns," he said.

He was a good brother. Ever since Flora had been adopted by the Kerr family, and come all the way from China to Ontario to live with them, Robert had been kind to her. Aunt May, who was Chinese, too, had helped arrange Flora's adoption. She had even gone with Mom to China to get four-year-old Flora. Her name had been Hoy Bit then. It meant Flower Honey. The Kerrs chose to change it to Flora, which meant "flower," and May after Aunt May, who had no little girl of her own.

But now Flora's face and her legs were aching with the cold, and the parade was taking hours to arrive.

"Here they come!" her brother cried. "I can hear the bands."

And right away, mobs of people shoved forward, pushing to get to where they could see better. Aunt May and Robert were both tall but Flora was not and, in no time, her view was totally blocked by the people pushing in front of her.

"Let my sister see," Robert told them, shoving some aside.

But just as a clown came dancing by, blowing kisses, a large lady moved into the space he had made and held her toddler up and told him to look. "The clown is waving to you, baby," she told her toddler. Then, backing up, she stepped squarely on Flora's left foot.

Nobody heard her yelp.

She had imagined her toes had lost all feeling, but she had been wrong.

She yanked her boot free, just as a band of men in kilts, all playing bagpipes, came marching past. Robert was laughing. He and Dad loved the noise of bagpipes. Flora wanted to cover her ears. She thought they sounded like creatures in torment.

"What's the matter?" Aunt May asked.

"Nothing," Flora said, smiling with gritted teeth.

"She doesn't like the bagpipes," Robert told Aunt May, "but they're gone now. You'll like the brass bands better, Flora."

She did, but she still wished she was somewhere else, somewhere warm where she could stop having to look at people's legs and backs.

Finally, Santa himself had ho-ho-hoed past them in his big sleigh, pulled by the reindeer, and it was time to have lunch and then go to Eaton's. She knew Robert planned to ask for a chemistry set, but she could not decide what she wanted.

When the waitress came to take their order, she asked Aunt May what her daughter would like. Flora and Aunt May smiled at each other. This had happened to them before and both of them liked it. Flora had no memory of her birth mother, who had put her in the orphanage when she was a baby, and Aunt May, who had wanted children, had none, so it was somehow comforting to be mistaken for mother and daughter.

"I'd like a grilled cheese sandwich," Flora said.

While they ate, she warmed up and her toes thawed out. But she was still tired when they headed downtown to Eaton's.

Robert got his chemistry set in no time, but Flora wandered up and down, unable to find something she longed for. Finally Aunt May grew impatient.

"How about one of these lovely dolls," she leaned down to urge. Flora was not keen on dolls, especially the ones Aunt May thought were so perfect. She looked up at them, standing in a long row of identical boxes. Wendy Walkers they were called. And every one was exactly the same as the one next to it.

"They can walk and talk," Aunt May was saying. "And just look at their clothes and their curls, Flora."

She was still going on about how special they were when Flora saw the one that was different. She was in the box at the very end of the row. But she was standing a little off-center and, instead of having her hands straight down at her sides like all the others, she had them stretched out toward Flora. It was only a little way out, but still it pleaded to be noticed. And her eyes seemed to be actually looking right into Flora's own.

"I want that one," Flora announced. "She is like the picture."

None of them understood at first. When the clerk reached up and took down the wrong doll, Flora almost had to yell before they heard her insist that she wanted not *that* one but the one on the end. She had to stamp her foot and get Robert to back her up before Aunt May gave in.

"I don't understand," Aunt May said, staring down at Flora's upset face.

"Flora's weird," Robert told them with a grin. "She won't change her mind or explain. You'd better just get her the one she wants if we are to catch the train."

When they got home, Flora had a hard time watching her doll being carried off by Aunt May, even though she knew she would be coming back on Christmas morning. But finally, the longed for moment arrived, and she unwrapped her new doll with enormous satisfaction.

Then, clutching it in her arms, she disappeared upstairs.

In all the Christmas bustle, everyone forgot about her until dinnertime. When she came to the table, Flora did not have her new doll with her but, busy eating the Christmas feast, nobody noticed.

Afterwards, when the Kerrs and their guests gathered in the

living room, Aunt May asked Flora to bring her Wendy Walker doll down to show them.

Flora hesitated a moment and then smiled.

"I'll get her," she said and vanished.

When she came back, she was carrying what looked like a different doll.

Aunt May looked at it and shook her head.

"I meant the new doll you chose that day at Toyland," she said. "The one that walks and talks and everything."

Flora held up the different doll.

"This is Harriet," she said. "She was with those Wendy Walkers, but she did not belong there. For one thing, she hates the name Wendy. Her name is really Harriet."

"Harriet!" Aunt May cried. "But Flora, what on earth is wrong with the name Wendy? It's the little girl in *Peter Pan*."

"I know," Flora said. "But my doll is not a Wendy. She's a Harriet. She's much happier with her right name. She told me so."

Robert looked at Aunt May's face and burst out laughing.

"I told you she's weird," he said. "I warned you when we were at the parade and she had a fit over the pipe band's music."

Flora gave her brother a withering look. Then she grinned at him.

"I cut her hair first," she said calmly, "so it wouldn't keep getting tangled. And I used Mother's sewing scissors and got out the things inside that made her do things she despises. She likes walking but not the way she used to, clunking along and jerking with every step. It looked so ugly. I made her glasses, too, out of pipe cleaners, but they keep falling off."

"But Flora, you've ruined her," Aunt May wailed.

"No, I didn't," Flora said. "Listen."

She held Harriet up in front of her and spoke.

"Harriet," she said, "why don't you say something to Aunt May."

She turned the doll around and Harriet said, in a clear small voice that sounded very real, "Merry Christmas, Aunt May. Thank you for saving me from being a Wendy Walker. Would you like to see me dance?"

Everyone was staring as Flora knelt and took Harriet's hands in hers. She sang, "Dance to your Mammy, my little lambie." And danced the doll around so that she kicked up her feet and finished off with a low bow.

"She can turn cartwheels, too," Flora said, "and tell stories and cuddle with me and read books. That Wendy Walker could only do things when you pulled her string or pushed the button in her back. But I just have to help Harriet a little bit, and she can do whatever she wants."

Dad was smiling, so that was all right. Flora looked at her mother then. Would she understand or was she as shocked as Aunt May?

She saw at once that, even though Mom was smiling at her, she also looked worried.

"Flora, you should have asked before you did such things to the new doll May bought for you," she said slowly.

Flora ducked her head down so that she was staring at the floor.

"You would have said 'No,'" she said, "and I had to save her. She was so unhappy there. Like me."

Then she dropped to her knees and buried her face in her mother's lap. They could all see her shoulders shake. She had started to cry. Nobody knew what to do.

Then Robert sprang up.

"I know why she did it," he announced. "It's that picture, isn't it, Flora?"

Before anyone could ask what he meant, he had rushed off to the bookcase in the next room and come back with the group photograph they had been sent from the orphanage in China. It showed a row of little girls, all standing stiffly, all dressed alike, all with their hair cut the same way, all wearing the same expression. There was only one who was different. It was the child at the end of the row. She was standing a little sideways and sucking her finger. Above her head, someone had marked an X to show this was Hoy Bit, the little girl the Kerrs were adopting. The unhappy little girl was Flora.

He passed the picture to Aunt May, knowing his mother had understood at once.

"They did look like that, those Wendy Walkers," he said. "Flora said something about the picture, but I didn't get it then."

Flora's head had come up. She stared at the brother who had explained it for her and nodded her head. Then, without another word, she took Harriet and walked her over to Aunt May. She perched the doll on the woman's knee.

Nobody spoke. They were all waiting for Flora's next move.

May cleared her throat and looked down at the barefoot little girl doll with chopped-off hair and the winning smile she had worn from the first.

"Are you happier now, Harriet?" she asked in a voice that shook.

"I am rapturous," Harriet said. "And you and Flora rescued me. Thank you for not being mad."

Aunt May lifted Harriet off her knee and hugged her. Then she looked from Robert to Flora. The tears on the little girl's cheeks had dried. Both their faces were alight.

"I did warn you she was weird," Flora's big brother said again.

"Not weird, Robert," May said softly. "Different or unique. Like this very merry Christmas we are having."

Scrap

Tim Jenks came limping down the stairs from the older boys' dormitory. He knew he was not a handsome youngster, with his rough shock of brown hair falling over his forehead, his too small eyes, his too wide mouth, and his sticky-out ears. He was "all elbows," as Matron said, and his right foot dragged. Yet, at this moment, the disability would not have been noticed by anyone catching sight of his sparkling eyes and the excitement that showed in every line of the lanky body. As he hustled down the narrow corridor leading to the entrance, Tim was hoping against hope that he would be in time.

Don't let him be gone, the boy prayed as he hobbled along.

He had his jacket and cap with him, just in case. He was about to enter the main hall when the sound of voices made him pause.

"My, it's cold tonight," Molly Band said.

Tim drew back. He did not want to spoil his chance by being caught eavesdropping. Why was Molly hanging about? She spoke again, sounding agitated.

"Oh, Dr. Barnardo, surely you aren't going out. Great men like you deserve to sit by their fireside on Christmas Eve."

Tim peeked around the corner and saw that Dr. Barnardo was shrugging into his greatcoat. If only Molly would take herself off!

"But Molly, if I hadn't gone out on Christmas Eve three years ago, I would not have found Tim Jenks unconscious in an alley."

"And I'd have died," Tim burst out, unable to stay hidden.

Molly jumped, but Tim could not waste time apologizing.

"Please, sir, let me come, too," he begged.

"How soon can you be ready?" Thomas Barnardo asked, winding his muffler around his neck and smiling at the eager boy.

"I'm ready now," Tim said, pulling on the jacket and cap. "I've even told Matron I'm going."

"If Matron says you're coming, it's settled," Barnardo said. "We'll leave the ninety-and-nine to sleep and go find a lost lamb."

"But it's Christmas Eve." Molly made a final protest.

"Where were the shepherds on the first Christmas Eve?" the man asked softly and led Tim out.

As the door shut, Tim came up with the answer and grinned. "Abiding in the fields, keeping watch over their flocks by night."

Had Molly got it? he wondered.

Tim and Thomas Barnardo prowled through the narrow, dank alleys of the slums for the next couple of hours, hunting for children with nobody to care for them and nowhere to shelter from the winter night. As they tramped through the wretched alleyways, Tim relived the night Barnardo had rescued him. Looking for someone who might give him a penny for bread, Tim had gone up to a group of young men, just as a fight broke out. He was knocked senseless, trodden on, and left for dead in a dark hole between two tenements. Barnardo had literally stumbled over his body as it was lying inert with snow sifting over it. An hour later, he would have been hidden from sight; an hour after that, he would have been dead. Thomas Barnardo had knelt and felt for a pulse. Finding the ten-year-old lived, he had taken him to a doctor.

Tim had had a fractured skull and a badly broken leg, and the surgeon had told Barnardo there was no hope. Tim had doggedly clung to life, however, and, upon regaining consciousness, he had set about changing his life. Now he could read and write and reckon up sums. He spoke much better English than he had known existed before coming to the Home. And he worshipped Thomas Barnardo.

Since then, he had often kept Barnardo company on his forays into the dark streets. He reassured boys who had learned the hard way not to trust anyone. Barnardo, touched by the boy's ardor, accepted his company, especially during the Christmas season, when the wretchedness they saw tempted him to despair.

"I know how it is for them," Tim told him. "I remember coming to and seeing you bending over me, looking at me as though I mattered. Nobody had ever looked at me that way before."

This night was one of the worst Tim had experienced. The two of them had to step over adults, sodden with gin, sprawled in doorways. Rats ran over the slimy paving stones. Once, they found themselves staring down at a dead baby, its wizened little face bluish and terrible. Tim realized his presence eased Barnardo's horror. The boy accepted such sights matter-of-factly, having seen it all before.

But Thomas Barnardo had spent an exhausting day, trying vainly to prove to several rich Londoners that his work was worthwhile. When midnight passed without either Tim or himself finding one lost lamb, he felt he could not go another step.

"Tim," he started to say, "maybe we should ..."

Tim pointed to a ladder leaning against the wall of a bakery.

"I've seen fellers go up here," he offered. "When they fire up the bake ovens, it's warm next to the chimneys. On such a cold night, there's prob'ly someone up there."

Barnardo, chilled and weary, stared at the ladder, which looked as though it had been knocked together years ago by a youth with no gift for carpentry. His reluctance was obvious.

"I'll run up and take a look myself, if you want to wait here," Tim said, longing to try one more cast.

DO NOT OPEN UNTIL CHRISTMAS

Again Barnardo recalled finding Tim. The boy would certainly have died from exposure if the man had gone home early.

"We'll both take a look," he grunted, doing his best to sound enthusiastic. After all, he was not fifty yet.

Tim raced up like a monkey. The doctor followed but he was heavier. A rotted rung gave under his boots and he had to spring to the next to avoid crashing to the pavement. Tim pulled him to safety.

Dr. Barnardo stood still for a second, catching his breath. Then he walked up to one of the great chimneys to check if any warmth lingered there. As he did so, his foot struck a heap of refuse. The next instant, man and boy discovered that the bundle of rags held a small, indescribably filthy child.

★

If Scrap had ever been given a name like other boys, he did not know it. Although today was his ninth birthday, he looked far more like a famished five-year-old. He ate bits of food he scrounged or stole. Scrap was a name that fitted him in every way.

He could not read. He rarely spoke. He was like a small, dirty, secretive animal who survives by keeping out of sight. About love, he knew nothing whatsoever. About joy, he was as ignorant as a stone.

As his eyes flew open, he saw a big boy with a triumphant grin.

"Oy!" Scrap yelped, thrusting aside the rags and starting to scramble to his feet.

But before he could escape, Tim had reached out like lightning and caught him by his bony shoulder. Scrap kicked and squirmed, but Tim hung on while Barnardo knelt by their captive and spoke quietly.

"We won't hurt you, lad," he said. "Trust me."

Scrap saw no reason to trust anyone, especially strangers who laid rough hands on his person.

"Lemme go," he whined, doing his best to bite Tim's hand.

"Would you like a hot meal, lad?" Barnardo asked, bending closer to make sure his offer was heard.

Scrap's mouth watered, but he still fought to get away. He had learned long since not to believe men when they offered food or lodging. They always wanted something in return.

"Tim," the man said quietly, "tell this scrap I won't harm him."

Scrap, startled at the use of his nickname, quit fighting and met the big boy's eyes. They were steady and strong, and looked as though he understood the younger boy's terror.

"Now then," Tim said. "Settle down, you little varmint. Dr. Barnardo won't harm you. I vouches for him, see."

"What do they call you?" the man asked.

"Scrap."

"Then hold still and listen to me, Scrap," the man said, giving the child a gentle shake. "I want to help you."

Hearing the name "Barnardo," Scrap blinked. He had heard rumors of this man. Some boys feared him. Others told of his saving friends of theirs. One boy had accused him of sending his brother to be a slave.

"Come on, Scrap. Ain't you hungry enough to eat a horse?" Tim said. "The Doctor won't harm you. If you takes off when you're full, he won't keep yer, as Gawd's my witness."

Scrap gave in. He could cut and run later if Tim was spinning him a yarn. Tim let go, reading his mind with ease.

"We'll take him home," Barnardo said, joyful over Scrap's rescue and longing for his own bed. "It's Christmas Day, Tim. There'll be goose and plum pudding tonight. Is Scrap your only name, child?"

Scrap eyed him uneasily. What was wrong with "Scrap"?

"Answer the gentleman, you," Tim ordered, giving him a friendly clout on the side of the head.

"Scrap's all the name I got," Scrap said hoarsely. Then his lips shut like a trap. That was all the jawing he planned on doing.

"Sir, here's a better way down," Tim said, pointing to the next building, which was so close to the bakery the eaves touched. There was a set of rough steps leading down to the street. Barnardo followed gratefully. He had thought he might have to stay stranded up here.

"Well done, Tim," he said. He went on casually, "I've known boys who didn't know their names. Scrap suits you."

Scrap was gratified but kept his face blank. He saw no need to comment. He was dreaming about plum pudding and goose, and his insides rumbled loudly. Neither of the others seemed to hear.

Scrap clambered into the hackney they summoned, determined

to keep a sharp eye on his rescuers, but he fell asleep in the warm interior of the cab. He woke when it jolted to a stop.

"Hop out," Tim ordered. "And no tricks, mind."

Scrap ignored this sally and stared at his new surroundings. The Barnardo Home was large and alarmingly like a fortress. The small boy was far too hungry by now to try running away. It was a severe shock to him when he was marched out to a scullery and told he had to have a bath before he ate. Barnardo went to summon help, but Tim kept a tight hold on the small boy.

"Not me! I never had a bath in me life," he objected.

"You don't have to tell me that," Tim told him with brutal candor. "You smells worse than a cesspit."

A brawny, sleepy-eyed woman, in a huge apron, ignored his protest. With Tim's able assistance, she stripped off his rags and plunged him in a tin tub filled with hot water.

"Lemme out!" Scrap shrieked, fighting like a mad thing.

"Hold still, you little bleeder," the woman said. "We're not enjoying this any more than you. I've seen plenty of dirty tykes dragged in here, but I think you take the prize."

Scrap was red as a boiled lobster before they were done. Even after the ordeal was over, he went on howling.

"Put his nightshirt on, Tim, while I fetch some food."

Tim, rubbing him dry, saw the child's body was not only terribly malnourished but covered with sores and bruises. Tim, who had arrived in much the same state three years earlier, became gentler as he plopped a flannel nightshirt over Scrap's damp head. The garment made Scrap's eyes stretch to their widest. He fingered the thick, soft material with reverence and searched in vain for holes or even worn spots. It was, to the boy, clothing fit for a king, and he was so staggered at having it put on him, that he was silent before the woman returned with bread and milk and a slice of cold meat.

Behind her came Dr. Barnardo, curious to see his latest find free of dirt, and Matron with her shears ready to cut off his hair.

Scrap, glimpsing them dangling at her waist, guessed what she was going to do and clapped his hands to his head, where his black hair was beginning to curl.

"You'll not cut it off," he screeched, jumping down from the stool and trying to elude them. "It's me only beauty. And it's mine!"

"She's got to get rid of the lice," Tim said reasonably, grabbing hold of a flying elbow. "You're crawling with them. But sit down first. Matron won't do it till you've had some food, will you, ma'am?"

"If he'll let me fine-comb it, I might not do it at all," she said, looking at the soft curls that adorned the small head. Without them, he would look like a shorn lamb ready for the butcher. "What curls!"

Scrap put up his hand to check. His curly mop, clean for the first time he could remember, grabbed at his exploring fingers, catching on the chapped places, clinging on as though it could not let go. He jerked his hands away and glared at the onlookers.

"Where's me dinner, then?" he demanded, sounding as brave and tough as he could manage.

"Here," Tim said understandingly. He took the bowl and set it on the table near Scrap's stool. "Set to."

Scrap's enormous eyes glistened as he gazed down at the stew. Then he fell upon it. There were hunks of meat that were not moldy or rancid. There were slices of carrot and potato, smothered in thick gravy. He started stuffing chunks into his mouth with both hands. Tim yanked away the dish and gave him a stern look.

"Slow down, you little blighter," he ordered sternly. "Can't yer see the spoon? If you pack it in so fast, your stomach won't be able to hold onto it and it'll come right back up. I've had to clean up a few messes from greedyguts like you. Now take it easy."

Scrap tried. It was very hard. He could not remember ever being given so much food before, good food, too. He returned Tim's scowl, picked up the spoon and, holding it awkwardly, began again.

"You're a good-looking scrap," Barnardo told him with a grin. "How old are you, do you know?"

"Nine," Scrap announced. "Nine today."

Although the words were indistinct, since his mouth was full, his pride was obvious. Many people in his world could not name their birthdays, but his age and date of birth were the two things he was sure of. Old Annie, who worked as a cook in an eating house, had told him she had seen him born.

"It was 1876, and cold as a tomb in that room," she said. "Yer maw said you was the best Christmas present your old man ever gave her. Usually he jist give her a black eye."

When Scrap had tried to learn more about his parents, Annie had shaken her head.

"Never knew her name," she said. "She died that same night, poor soul. Meg Winker took you and fed you, her just having lost a babe, but she died, too, before you were big enough to be much use to her. I've always been surprised you found yourself enough food to stay alive, but you're a cunning little bastard. Tough as a boot."

He saw her a time or two after that and hoped to get more information, until she, too, vanished without trace. Still, he held onto the knowledge that he was born on Christmas Day and, each Christmas that passed, he knew he grew a year older.

"Nine—and he looks five or six," Dr. Barnardo muttered.

Scrap ignored this. He was, to his own astonishment, too full to eat another bite, even though there was still a little milk left. He patted his stomach to make sure and found it stretched tight as a drum. Matron went to work on his hair with a special comb. He sat there in a daze, crying out when she pulled. He was falling asleep where he sat. The tangles defeated her at last, and she ended up cutting it short all over but allowing him to keep a couple of inches. What was left curled up tightly like a snug cap and made him look far more attractive than anyone seeing him an hour before would have thought possible.

Suddenly he yawned so widely his jaws cracked. Still perched on the stool, he started to sway.

"Bed for you," Matron said, "before you topple over. Come on."

When Scrap woke, he was covered with a blanket, which he jerked up to just below his big, dark eyes. He almost hid himself completely under its folds, but he was too afraid. What if someone, or Something, crept up and grabbed him while he was unable to see?

✴

"Who're you?" a voice demanded.

Scrap turned his head carefully to inspect the owner of the voice. It was a boy with bright blue eyes, a thatch of red hair, and a black scowl. Scrap looked away fast. The other boy was big, and he seemed all set to pounce on a newcomer. Scrap did not speak.

"Aw, it's a new one. You know what they're like. Who brought you in, kid? Barnardo himself with Tim? Or somebody else?"

Scrap turned his head again. The second speaker was the same size as the first. His fair hair was about an inch long all over his squarish head. His eyes were brown and he looked not unfriendly. But Scrap decided, since there were two of them, he'd better answer.

"Tim and the doctor," he mumbled. "I'm Scrap."

"They'll soon change that," the first boy said. "Everyone called me Tyke before I come here. Now I'm supposed to be Thomas. Can you beat that?"

"Watch it, Tyke. Thomas is the doctor's name. I'm Nathan," the other boy volunteered. "My ma called me Nathan after me uncle. She's dead, but at least she named me right and proper."

"What else do they do to you here?" Scrap forced out the words.

"They feed you and clean you and pray over you and give you a name, if you haven't one. Then some boys get sent to Canada. Some get 'prenticed. My cousin got to be a blacksmith's boy. He's up north somewhere now."

Scrap felt confused, but any question he might have asked was broken off as a bell set up a deafening clamor. The others sprang out of bed and ripped Scrap's blanket off.

"Up, you." Thomas grinned at him. "It's time to stir yer stumps. If you want breakfast ..."

Scrap almost smiled.

Yet, those first days, Scrap almost ran away several times. It was the thought of dinner that held him. Shepherd's pie and beef stew. He got new clothes, the same as every other boy's. He was told he would be attending school.

That first Christmas morning, he went to church for the first time in his life. He would have been terrified if it had not been for Thomas and Nathan sitting next to him. Tim sat right behind him. He knew, although he would never have said so, that if it had not been for his insistence, Scrap would not have been found. It made the small boy seem especially his, as though they were almost brothers.

Scrap was enthralled by the Christmas story. A woman, long ago, had had a baby in a stable. Scrap pictured the livery stable, where he had been tossed a penny every so often for holding somebody's horse. It was not a nice place to give birth, any more than the backroom of the slum where the old woman had said he had been born. Nobody had been ready for the first Christmas baby, either.

"And she called his name Jesus," the minister read out in his deep plummy voice.

Why on earth did she call him that? Scrap wondered, shocked. He had heard the words "Jesus Christ" used as swear words. He had no idea that Christ was also in the word Christmas. He listened to the story of the shepherds, the angels, the star, and the three kings.

Well, he thought, Jesus isn't going to be my name, whatever the doctor says. Scrap will do me fine.

He liked the sound of the word Christmas, though. He liked its link to his mother and his birthday and his rough entrance into the world. There was something in the story the minister read that seemed to say this Jesus did not know his father's name, either. And Tim had said he, too, had been found on Christmas. Scrap had not felt safe often in his short life, but he did feel safe with Tim.

"If you don't want to call me Scrap, call me Christmas," he told Dr. Barnardo that afternoon, when the man asked him once again if Scrap was his only name.

"Christmas?" Thomas Barnardo said, staring down at him. "What on earth made you think of such a thing?"

Scrap was still not used to talking. He set his jaw.

"I'm Scrap," he said. "But if you needs more, Christmas is it."

"We'll settle for Scrap," the doctor said.

But long before bedtime, everyone in the Home knew that Scrap had called himself Christmas. This strange choice, the fact that he had come to them on Christmas, and his small size endeared him to everyone.

Scrap had the same problems all new boys had at Dr. Barnardo's Home. He stole food when he got the chance.

"You don't need to steal grub," Tim told him quietly. "I know it's hard to believe, but the food here won't ever give out. If you stay, you'll never go hungry again."

"How're yer so sure?" Scrap asked.

"Because I did the same thing when he brought me here three years ago. And I've never once missed a meal."

"All right, Tim," Scrap said, and no more food left the dining hall tucked under his shirt.

He swore and had to have a severe talking-to from Matron. Once Tim convinced her that the words had no meaning for Scrap, she started in on his education. He had to learn to use a knife and fork, comb his hair, clean his teeth, use a napkin, shine his shoes, be moderately polite, and never to take the name of the Lord in vain.

He found it a great strain, obeying so many ridiculous rules.

"I kin always run away. If Matron says just once more, 'Scrap, hold that fork properly,' I'm off."

Tim heard this and felt a startling desolation.

"Don't talk that way," he said roughly. "You can't leave."

"Why not?" demanded Scrap indignantly.

"We got found on Christmas," Tim said slowly, knowing he was not telling the real reason. "So we're like ... like brothers. You can't go off without me, see?"

Scrap stared at him. Then he ducked his head.

"I didn't mean it, Tim," he said with a gulp.

Tim told himself he only watched out for Scrap because he was so small and, after all, he had been responsible for finding him. The fact was, he hungered for someone to love as he had long ago loved his own older brother. Dick had been taken off by the press gang when he was fifteen and Tim was seven. Until he was ten, Tim had lived from hand to mouth. Nobody had cared tuppence for him until Barnardo pulled him from the snow. Now Barnardo was his hero, but he needed someone like himself to love. Scrap filled the empty place.

✱

Soon it was time for the next group of Barnardo children to leave for Canada. Scrap was undersized. The Canadian farmers who took in Barnardo boys wanted lads who could help with farm labor.

"I've been told there are people who want to adopt boys as

family members," Dr. Barnardo mused. "Somebody over there must be waiting for our Scrap."

Matron was not so sure.

"He's stronger now. Cocky, too. How about Tim Jenks? He's taken Scrap under his wing. He'll miss him sorely if he's sent away."

"I know. It took Tim so long to heal. Then I admit I grew used to his being here. But he must have his chance. Let's send them both."

Matron had heard some hard facts about the homes where some of their children had gone. But surely nobody could be cruel to Scrap.

Believing, like all the Barnardo children, that Canada was the Promised Land, Scrap was overjoyed to hear he was going on the same ship as his friends, Nathan and Tyke.

When Barnardo told Tim that he, too, was going to Canada, the boy was torn. His eyes grew moist and his lip trembled.

"I don't want to leave you," he faltered, "but ..."

"You must go along to keep an eye on Scrap or he'll be sure to fall overboard." Barnardo tried for a bantering tone.

Tim's misery visibly lightened.

"I could lend a hand with him," he said. "He likes me."

The night before they left, none of the boys could get to sleep.

"My big brother said there are wolves there," Nathan said into the darkness. "And tigers."

"Wolves maybe, but no tigers," Tyke declared. "I asked Matron."

"What did she say, exactly?" Nathan asked, still inclined to believe his older brother.

"She laughed at the very notion. Polar bears, she said, and bogey men who chased bad boys to eat them alive. But no tigers."

"Bogey men ..." Scrap quavered.

"Aw, she was teasing. She's forever on about those old bogey men," Tyke said, no hint of a quaver in his easy laughter.

"Maybe we ought ter pray," Scrap whispered after a pause.

Tim, called upon to lead them, swallowed hard and repeated the Lord's Prayer in a droning voice. Then he burst out, "Be with us, God, when we're so far from home."

Nobody questioned his use of the word "home." They knew where home was, just as Tim himself did.

✳

The boys bound for Canada were each given a trunk containing new clothes and a Bible. Carrying these proudly, they marched onto the ship. Mr. Marsh and Mrs. Blackstone were in charge of them. Both were strict but fair, keeping to the schedule they had been given and making sure their charges obeyed the rules. Once the ship set sail, most of the boys were seasick. Bringing up his boots, Scrap wished he had stayed behind. But on the third day out, he woke up to find he was actually hungry for breakfast. They were kept busy on the voyage. They had prayer meetings every day, listening to sermons, singing hymns and songs like "Rule, Britannia," repeating scripture and prayers they had memorized. They did exercises, ran races, played games, and discussed what their lives would be like once they got to the land they had been told would be full of promise. Tim was kept busy rescuing them from trouble.

Finally someone saw land and a cheer went up. Herded onto a train bound for Toronto, Tim Jenks's group was eager to see what Canada was really like. As the train chugged across the miles, the boys pressed their noses against the dusty windows, looking for wheat fields and wild animals. Nothing was quite as they had imagined before they left England, but everything they saw fascinated them.

Once they arrived in Toronto, they went to a place in the city, until requests came in for home boys to go to farms near Guelph. Mr. Atkins, from the Barnardo home in Toronto, came with them to make sure they arrived safely. He was a big man, who kept counting them but was not ready to answer their questions. They climbed onto the train, laughing and pushing each other, while Mr. Atkins kept telling them to behave themselves.

They were far too excited to settle down. None of them had ever lived outside a big city. Not one of them had ever seen a cow or even weeded a garden.

When they got off the train, eleven of them stood huddled together on the Guelph station platform, waiting to meet the people who had asked for boys to work on farms.

"Hey, Tim, what will they want us to do?" Scrap asked. He had asked before, so he knew Tim was not sure, but he needed to hear his friend's voice.

"We'll find out when we get there," Tim told him again.

Tyke and Nathan were taken first by one couple, who laughed at their scared expressions and gave them gingerbread to eat in the buggy.

Then the others began to be driven away, one by one. Tim skulked at the back, unwilling to go until he saw Scrap safe. Finally, there were only the two of them left. As Mr. Atkins looked like he was giving up, a woman reined in her horse and stared at the group with anxious eyes.

"Do you come to get a Home boy, madam?" Mr. Atkins asked.

Scrap, feeling the lady's glance on him, clutched Tim's hand.

"Are they brothers?" she demanded. "I don't want two."

"No, madam. I doubt the little chap will be much use to you, but the big boy's strong, despite his limp."

"Oh, I couldn't take a cripple. My brother told me to get a healthy boy who'd be useful. The smaller one would be better."

Tim's grief at leaving Scrap, and his shame at being called "a cripple," made him look sullen. But Scrap, who was thin and pale, did not look as though he could be of much use. Mr. Atkins stared at the woman and shook his head. "I'm afraid you are making a mistake, madam," he told her, not glancing at either of the boys.

"I can see he isn't strong, but he can help me until he grows stouter," she said, her chin up, her cheeks red. "It won't take much to feed such a scrap."

"Tim," Scrap cried, "don't let me go."

"I can't help it. You go on now," Tim said, in a helpless rage. "I promise I'll come and see you. What's your name, missus?"

The woman hesitated.

"Mrs. Fiddler," she said at last. "What's the lad's name?"

"Scrap," Scrap himself said, as Tim boosted him into the gig and Mrs. Fiddler told the horse to "gidd-up." She did not look back or give Scrap a chance to say goodbye.

Craning his neck to see, Scrap watched a big carriage pull up to the station as they left. The people in it were smiling. There was a boy about Tim's age.

They would be sure to like Tim.

An icy lump had settled in Scrap's stomach. He felt more alone than he had felt in all his years as a street child. If only he had not come to love Tim, he would not be lonely now ...

He turned forward again, keeping his head down. The woman, watching him, knew he was fighting to keep back tears. She recognized that struggle. Since James had died, leaving her penniless, and she had had no choice but to go back to her brother's home, she had cried herself to sleep every night.

When she drove in, her brother was standing on the front stoop.

His slate-gray, flint-hard eyes raked Scrap's body from scuffed boot toes to black curls. Scrap knew, at once, that Mrs. Fiddler feared this man. He longed to jump down and run, but everything was too strange, and he would never be able to find Tim.

"Was that the best you could do?" Jethro White drawled. Even though he did not speak loudly, there was menace in his words. His sneering look cut like the flick of a lash. Scrap felt Mrs. Fiddler wince.

"Scrap's a good boy," she said feebly. "He can help me with my chores until he puts on weight. There was nobody else left."

There was Tim, Scrap thought, but he kept quiet.

"Scrap? Is that the sort of name they give these little tramps? He looks like an organ grinder's monkey. Are you Eyetalian, boy?"

Scrap swallowed. He had no idea what to say. He knew nothing about his parents. He himself had been born in Three Farthing Lane, but he sensed that he should not say so.

"Answer me when I speak to you, boy, or you'll get a taste of my belt before you're a day older."

"I don't know," Scrap faltered.

"He'll steal everything if we let him in the house. He can sleep in the woodshed."

"Jethro, there's no ..."

"You're satisfied with the woodshed, ain't you, Scrappy?" the man demanded.

"Yes," Scrap said mechanically.

"Yes, Mr. White, you mean. You look sickly. Did you catch some disease on the boat?"

"No, Mr. White."

Then Mrs. Fiddler motioned for him to jump down. She herself climbed wearily to the ground and began to lead the horse into the stable. Scrap went to help. Horses he knew something about. Out of the corner of his eye, he saw the man stare at the two of them a few seconds longer. Then he limped inside, slamming the door.

When the woman and boy were leading the horse into his stall in the barn, she moved close to Scrap and began to whisper a hasty story.

"Our father was cruel to my brother when we were children," she told the boy. "He was forever beating him and blaming him for anything that went wrong. It made Jethro hard. Then he was run over on the road and the injury left him lame. I should have known not to bring you home, child. I should have realized how it would be."

Scrap did not know what to say but, remembering the way the man's cold eyes had looked him over, he shivered.

The two of them came to the barn door without speaking. Then the woman said, "I knew I shouldn't bring you here—but it gets so lonely."

They walked to the house in silence. White had come back out.

"That Eyetalian monkey means to kill us in our beds and then run back to his pals," he snarled, as though Scrap were not within earshot. "Well, I've put a lock on the woodshed and there's no window he can wriggle through. I'll turn the key on him before I go to bed."

"What if there's a fire …?" his sister began.

"Good riddance," he said and smiled at the horror in her eyes.

He put Scrap to work at once, shoveling out the manure from the horse's stall. Supper was a brief, meager meal: dry bread, some chunks of raw turnip and a cup of water. Afterward, when the man went to talk to a neighbor about something, his sister slipped an apple into Scrap's hand. When it was too dark for Scrap to do anything more, White showed him the woodshed. Scrap was not given a candle, but the man held his aloft so the boy could see that there was no bed in the small, musty place, just a heap of straw.

"It's a palace compared to those hovels they're forever telling us about," Jethro White said with a grating laugh.

He shoved Scrap through the door and turned the key.

The next day, Alice Fiddler managed to slip him a worn sheepskin to lay between his body and the prickly straw. Scrap knew that even that small gift took courage.

✳

Waiting for Tim to keep his promise, Scrap stuck it out for the next four months. His life during that time was a nightmare. He had suffered before but not from cold, deliberate brutality. He was beaten for every mistake he made and many he did not. He was not given enough to eat and, often, even the sparse, unappetizing food was withheld due to some manufactured sin. The insults grew in intensity. Scrap knew that some of this abuse was aimed at Alice Fiddler. It was clear that her brother enjoyed seeing her cringe and hearing her beg. But the knowledge was no help.

It was weeks before he learned that Tim was unlikely to find the farm by asking for Mrs. Fiddler, since the place belonged to Jethro. Not knowing what to do, Scrap endured, waiting for a rescue that never came.

At last, Mrs. Fiddler grew ill and Jethro, much against his will, had to send for the doctor.

"Go to your sister in Arthur and stay until you're better, or you'll be dead before spring," the doctor said, giving Jethro a look of disgust.

She left on the morning of Christmas Eve, but although Scrap knew vaguely that December had come, there was no air of celebration at the Whites'. The boy was too bruised in body and spirit to realize that his birthday was only hours away.

"I can get some real work out of you with her gone," Jethro White exulted.

That night, he beat Scrap savagely and then began drinking. By ten o'clock, he had sunk into a stupor. Scrap found him passed out on the kitchen floor. The boy gazed down at the man, who was breathing heavily and drooling from one corner of his open mouth. He would not come to for hours.

This is my chance, he thought desperately. *I have to take it.*

Tim had never found him. Barnardo was across the sea, saving slum children, unconcerned about his lambs in Canada. Nobody cared what became of Scrap. If he died in the snow, it would not matter.

Still, when he went back to the woodshed to get the chunk of bread he had hidden under the straw, he picked up the sheepskin Alice Fiddler had given him. He wondered where the man had put the trunk sent out with every Barnardo boy, but he did not stop to look for it. He just wanted to be gone.

He came close to dying from exposure within the next few hours. It was snowing and a wind was driving the sharp flakes at anyone foolish enough to be out in the night. No matter which way he walked, the wind always seemed to be aimed at his face. Afraid he might be discovered, he stowed away in the back of a farm wagon, while its owner stopped off at a house. When the man returned, the boy jolted along for miles without being spotted. As the wagon slowed and turned in at the owner's farm lane, Scrap slid off the back and ducked into a nearby clump of evergreens. If the family's dog had been abroad, he would have been caught, but the man's wife had taken pity and let the collie into the warm kitchen.

Scrap trudged on down the road a short distance. In a church steeple, a bell had begun to ring in Christmas Day, but he barely heard it. He was growing sleepy and, soon now, he was going to lie down. He would die, he knew, but it did not matter. He was so tired and Tim had never come.

He slumped down against a half-buried fence post and was letting himself drift into the slumber that would end all his pain and weariness, when he heard a sound. It was something unexpected. It was a sound he knew. It was the bleat of a lost lamb.

He pulled the stiffened sheepskin up over his head but he still heard it. He had cared for Jethro White's poor flock and had learned something of sheep during his months in Canada. That lamb was very young. It sounded newborn.

Why didn't it go to its dam?

Maybe it hasn't a mother, he thought gropingly. Maybe it's an orphan. Tim would try to save it.

It bleated again. But this time, the cry was weaker.

In spite of himself, Scrap staggered onto his feet and set out to follow the pitiful bleating.

It seemed to take hours but, really, he discovered the tiny black lamb in a very few minutes. It was lying next to its mother, but the mother was dead.

"Your Ma died that same week." Was that what the old woman had told him?

He lifted the tiny creature, wrapped it in the sheepskin to protect it, and set out, hugging it to him. A long way away, in the next big field, he could see a barn. If he could get her that far, he might be able to save her.

Help me, he begged the wind. Help me.

They warmed each other, Scrap and the newborn creature hugged tight against him, as he ploughed through the thigh-high drifts, making for the barn. He fell twice, but neither he nor the lamb was injured. At last, he reached the big door. Would he be able to get it open? His fingers had so little feeling in them by now.

But as he stretched out his numb hand, the big door opened by itself and a boy came out. He was a big boy, wrapped in warm clothes. The thick muffler hid his face.

"I got a lamb," Scrap told the boy.

Then, unable to say another word, he toppled over at Tim Jenks's feet.

When Tim reached the house, carrying both lambs in his arms, nobody believed it at first. All the festivity Jethro White's place lacked was in the Gordons' fragrant, candlelit kitchen. Evergreen boughs festooned every ledge, and the air was filled with the smells of baking. But all of this was forgotten, as Tim bore Scrap and the lamb over to the settle by the hearth.

When the family learned the child in his arms was Scrap, the boy Tim had told them about, the child they had been seeking for months, they exclaimed it was a miracle. They removed the lamb to a box kept for such little ones and wrapped Scrap in warm blankets. He was given a sip of Hamish's Scotch whiskey, and then a bowl of hot barley soup was spooned into him.

One of the grandchildren gave the lamb some milk and another piped, "Let's name the lamb Christmas." Only Scrap heard Tim laugh.

They were enraged when they saw the bruises on the small boy's face and his body, which was nothing but skin and bone. He gazed at their angry eyes and knew he had been wrong about nobody caring what happened to him. These strangers cared.

"You'll never have to go back, not for one moment," Elspeth Mary Gordon said fiercely.

Scrap dozed then, until he heard an old lady called Ailsa say, "The Lord must have saved you."

"No," Scrap mumbled, rousing himself to set her straight. "It was Dr. Barnardo ... and Tim."

Tim held him close within the circle of his arm. Scrap saw that, although his friend's cheeks were wet, he was smiling at him, the boy whom he had found on a bakeshop roof a year ago this very night.

"It's the same thing," Tim said quietly, "and now you've done it, too."

"Done what?" Scrap murmured, so sleepy he doubted he'd hear the answer.

"Abided in the fields," said Tim Jenks, "keeping watch over your flock by night."

Ten Lords a-Leaping, Nine Ladies Dancing

When Grandma fell, coming out of church after the Advent Service, Olivia was horrified. But it was not until after her grandmother had gone to the hospital that she had found out that Gran had a concussion and a badly broken arm.

"I am sorry," her grandfather told her, "but you'll have to go stay with your cousin Esther until your grandmother can come home."

Olivia hardly knew Cousin Esther.

"Couldn't we manage …?" she had started to ask. But she had read the answer in her Grandpa's face. If she hadn't been stuck in a wheelchair, it would have been possible. But Olivia was unable to walk, and Grandpa would have to do the farm chores and visit his wife in the hospital, as well as cook for himself. She was only twelve. He could not look after her and do everything else. She would have to go.

As he wheeled her up to the Bridgmans' door, Olivia knew she was going to be miserable. She had only met this Cousin Esther twice. The woman was not used to looking after handicapped kids. And Olivia, having listened in on Grandpa's phone call, knew she was not happy about Olivia's coming.

"I'll be back to get you in no time," her grandfather said, leaning down to kiss her goodbye. "You have fun with your cousins, honey."

"Oh, she will," Cousin Esther gushed, beaming at him. "Julia and her friends are having a party to celebrate finishing their lessons in ballroom dancing. The night after tomorrow this place will be positively bouncing!"

Grandpa's eyes met Olivia's, and they both knew he was sorry he had to leave her. Then he was gone.

Before Olivia could move, Cousin Esther started propelling her down the hall to the room where she would be sleeping. As they sped along, her cousin chattered, telling Olivia over and over again how pleased she was when Olivia's grandfather had asked her to take Olivia in.

A couple of times, Olivia opened her mouth to answer but then, as the torrent of words kept flooding over her, she finally understood that no replies were needed.

At last, the visitor was helped to get ready for bed and then tucked in.

When she was alone, Olivia burst into silent tears, but she soon found crying didn't help. After a couple of minutes, she mopped her wet face on the sheet. Then, lying still in the darkness, she heard her cousin Julia come home.

Olivia listened while Julia's mother told her daughter about Olivia's being there.

Then mother and daughter launched into what sounded like a shouting match. Every so often, Cousin Esther would hush Julia but, always, Olivia heard the bruising words before the girl was told to lower her voice.

"Mother, how could you have let her come? She's a baby and she's crippled. She won't fit in at the party," stormed the girl. "We're going to dance, remember? She can't even stand up!"

"Julia, stop," Cousin Esther broke in, but Julia wasn't finished.

"And we can't leave her out, not when she's right here in the house. Why, oh, why didn't you tell him it was impossible?"

In the dark bedroom, Olivia cringed as she heard her cousin bemoaning her inability to dance.

"Do hush, Julia," Cousin Esther begged. "She'll hear you."

"I bet she's asleep," the sulky voice grumbled.

Then, without warning, Julia broke out with an announcement that she came close to shouting.

"I haven't even told you the amazing news. Noreen's brother Chris might drop in. He's in university. He's twenty, Mom, and so good looking. He's a guy to die for."

"Really, Julia, what a thing to say! But it is lovely that he's coming."

"Not with dreary little Olivia sitting in the corner, putting a damper on everything. Why you had to agree to her coming this week … really, Mother."

"I couldn't help it," Cousin Esther burst out at last. "I had no choice when Olivia's grampa called. Julia, just put yourself in my place."

Rage boiled up inside Olivia. She told herself she didn't care, but it wasn't true. Julia was horrible and so was her mother. Olivia decided she would tell them she had a headache tomorrow and she would stay in her room with the door shut. Julia would pretend to be ever so sorry, but she'd be singing Hallelujahs inside.

That night, Olivia dreamed about the accident again. She almost always did when she went to bed feeling unhappy. She and her mother and father had been in a car crash when she was five. Her parents had been killed, and she had suffered a spinal injury that left her paralyzed. After she was released from the rehab hospital, she had gone to live with her grandparents on their small farm in Muskoka.

It had been quiet there and peaceful. Olivia remembered how, bit by bit, she had become herself once more. She had learned to read, and she had helped care for their animals. When they got her the wheelchair, she had grown more independent. And lately, Gran had started teaching her to cook.

When she woke up that first morning, she managed to get herself partway dressed. Taking her socks and shoes in her lap, she wheeled to the kitchen where Cousin Esther was setting the breakfast table.

"My gracious," the woman cried, staring at Olivia. "I was coming to get you up in a jiffy. Can I help you with those things?"

Olivia smiled at her. She could see that Cousin Esther, underneath her welcoming beam, was nervous. Lots of people got that way when they first met a handicapped girl. Olivia knew how to help them over it.

"I'm used to getting myself up, but I do need a hand," she explained.

Cousin Esther had just finished doing up her shoe when, all at once, Julia came bursting in.

"Did you bring a party dress?" she demanded.

"Julia, where are your manners?" her mother objected. "At least say good morning to your cousin before you start bombarding her with questions."

Olivia ignored this. Her eyes met Julia's straight on.

"No," she said quietly. "I don't own what you'd call a party dress. I'm just twelve. You must be sixteen."

She knew Julia was not quite fifteen, and she saw the flattery had worked. Julia was definitely pleased to be mistaken for somebody that much older.

"I don't think Grandpa realized you were having a party," she added.

"We can find a dress for her," Cousin Esther said. "Maybe one of yours would do. She's smaller than you are. That pretty rose-colored one with the little white flowers on it should fit her."

"I guess so," Julia said, helping herself to a bowl of cereal. "She sure couldn't wear what she's got on now."

"Oh, Julia, don't be rude. Olivia looks fine for a morning at home. You're not fancied up yourself," her mother snapped.

Olivia spread jam on the toast Cousin Esther passed her. In no time, she could escape with her book. She was sure Julia would not object.

And she was absolutely right. Julia no sooner finished eating than she was on the phone, calling the first of a list of friends.

Cousin Esther came out of a closet with Julia's party dress and insisted Olivia try it on at once. Julia, looking impatient but curious, came to watch. Olivia guessed she was wondering how a "crippled" girl would manage, but she kept her expression blank and got on with it. The dress was pretty and it fit her perfectly, which was a relief to them all. As soon as she had gotten out of it, Olivia declared that she had a book she wanted to finish.

"Oh, what is it?" Cousin Esther asked, but she did not wait to be told.

Olivia opened *Emily of New Moon* and pretended to be so caught up in it, she did not know what was going on around her. After lunch, a mob of girls came over to help Julia decorate. They hung up rainbow streamers and bright balloons. There were silver and gold wreaths, and everything was sprayed with sparkle. There was much laughter when Julia climbed a stepstool to fasten a sprig of mistletoe above the door.

DO NOT OPEN UNTIL CHRISTMAS

Olivia watched Christmas get buried under the party decorations. Even the tree looked changed into a different thing. Instead of the angel that topped the tree at the farm, Cousin Esther pinned up a silver whirligig that spun with every passing breeze. It looked in danger of tipping, but Olivia liked it.

Luckily, the living room was huge. When Julia had pushed the furniture aside, there would be plenty of space for dancing.

Olivia did her best to stay out of the way but, although Julia would have supported her, Cousin Esther made both girls uncomfortable as she kept reminding them that Olivia was their guest and must be treated as such.

Olivia had trouble keeping the girls' names straight. There were Ashley and Courtney, Doreen and Noreen, Janice and Misty. When Olivia found a corner into which she could retreat, Noreen saw the book on her lap and came over to see what it was.

"*Emily of New Moon*," she said. "I love that story. Have you read the sequels?"

"I brought them with me," Olivia told her. "I haven't finished this one yet."

Noreen sat down beside her.

"They're not as good," she said. "I'm glad I read them, I guess, but I didn't like the endings."

Julia paused to glance down at them.

"Noreen is as bad as you, Olivia," she said. "She's always got her nose in a book. But she has a very nice brother, who said he'd come tomorrow. Do you think he really will, Norry?"

Noreen laughed.

"He'll come, but I am not promising that he'll stay more than five seconds," she said. "Though he might, once he finds out there's a bookworm here. Chris is as bad as I am. He's read all the *Harry Potter* books twice and *The Lord of the Rings* over and over."

Julia gave a snort.

"Come help decorate," she said.

Noreen grinned at Olivia.

"She thinks she's queen for the night," she murmured, getting up to go.

Grandpa called that evening.

"Margery is quite herself again," he said, chuckling. "They're sending her home tomorrow. So I'll be coming to fetch you the next day."

Olivia cheered. When she hung up the receiver, she saw Cousin Esther and Julia staring at her. She couldn't believe they minded, but they both looked hurt. And she couldn't think of anything she might say to fix things.

Finally, she just smiled and said, "It was so great to hear his voice. And to know that Grandma's well enough to come home."

Cousin Esther beamed at that, and Julia's face seemed to relax. Olivia bent her head over her book again, wondering if she had imagined they had actually been wounded by her cheering.

The next afternoon, all the girls came over. After a hurried pizza supper, they rushed to change. Then they all put on make-up. This was not easy, since there was only one large well-lit mirror. They also kept giggling and teasing each other. Olivia, who had never been one of such a group, watched in fascination. She was dressed up, too, of course. When she glimpsed herself in the mirror, she could feel herself blush. She didn't look like her everyday self in Julia's dress.

"That dress looks great on you, Olivia," Julia said, looking her over. She smiled and added, "Better than it ever looked on me."

Olivia was taken aback but pleased. She was relieved when Noreen drew her away. As they talked, Olivia learned that the other girl's family had a cottage on Lake Rosseau.

"That's near our farm," Olivia told her.

"We always go up for New Year's," Noreen said. "Maybe we could get together."

Olivia stared at her. Was she serious?

"I'll ask my mom," Noreen said, and went to help choose the perfect dance music. They had done this earlier in the day, but Julia said it was not what they needed to set the mood.

Olivia was back in her corner when the doorbell rang and the boys crowded in. She sat quietly, studying the newcomers. A couple were good looking but several had acne. Some were just small and sort of weedy. One, when he spoke, lisped and another boy squeaked. They were uneasy at first. But Julia, who had relaxed once they were all present, was kind to them. As she made them laugh, their nervousness soon wore off. Watching her, Olivia decided she wasn't horrible, after all.

It was close to ten o'clock when the bell rang one last time and everyone stiffened. The girls stood in a ragged line, staring at the opening door. Their eyes were wide, their mouths agape. Olivia bit back a giggle.

"It's your brother, Noreen," Julia said, her voice shaking wildly.

And then, there he was, tall and handsome, sweeping in, his face alight with laughter.

Until that moment, Olivia had not realized that, in choosing her hideaway spot, she had placed her wheelchair directly opposite the door through which the guy to die for must come. Believing he would have no reason to notice her, Olivia was completely relaxed as she watched him enter.

But his sparkling blue eyes lit upon her at once, and he flabbergasted everyone as he strode across the floor, bowed low in front of Olivia and said, "May I have the honor of this dance?"

Julia probably did not mean to speak so loudly when she blurted out, "But Olivia can't dance …"

Chris ignored her. He had taken hold of the arms of Olivia's chair and whirled her out into the middle of the room. He shot a look at

Julia, then that made her back up a step. The others automatically followed her lead.

Then Chris was grinning down at Olivia.

"She's doing just fine, aren't you, Olivia?" he said, smoothly. "My sister told me about you. You're the one who reads."

Olivia nodded. She could feel that her cheeks were on fire and her eyes were shining. It couldn't be true but it was. Noreen's brother, the twenty-year-old college student, the boy who loved to read, had chosen to dance with her. She had thought Julia was right about her being unable to do it, but he was giving her wheelchair wings.

He told her later about being a counselor at Woodeden, a camp for children with disabilities. That was where he had learned how to make a wheelchair twirl. He danced with the others, even Julia. But before he left, he came back to Olivia and gave her two extra turns.

"Have you read Terry Pratchett's books?" he had asked her.

And she had nodded and told him she especially liked the ones about the gnomes.

When they had all gone and it was time for bed, Julia stared down at her cousin. Then she grinned. "How did you like being the belle of the ball?" she teased.

Olivia gaped at her, unable to come up with an answer.

"You can keep the dress," Julia said then. "You will probably be needing it."

Olivia pulled herself together and smiled back at her.

"Thanks a lot," she said. "I think it's a once-in-a-lifetime dress, but one never knows."

And as she wheeled herself into the bedroom, she realized suddenly that she would actually miss Julia when she was back with her grandparents in the quiet farmhouse. She was happy to be going home. They would be together again on Christmas Day. But it would not be as exciting as life at Cousin Esther's. It wasn't Julia's fault that Olivia had gate-crashed her party and, once she had gotten used to the idea, things had been fine.

Then she wondered if Noreen would really call. She hoped so.

She was packing her bag, when she saw the party dress hung over the back of a chair. She stared at it for a moment. Then she wheeled across and took it with her to the suitcase she had brought, folded it as flat as she could manage, and hid it in the bottom, under her sensible clothes and books. They always had guests for Christmas dinner. Grandpa had said they would this time, too. He had told people to bring potluck, and the minister's wife was cooking a turkey.

She would put the party dress on when they weren't looking, and appear in it when they called her.

Maybe her legs were paralyzed, but Chris had danced with her. And on Christmas Day, when her family beheld her, her heart would be dancing.

It was dancing already.

How Barney Saved the Day

The phone ringing wakened Barney. He lay still, sure somehow that it was too late for phone calls. He heard his mother cry out then. His eyes opened wide at the tension in her voice. He stayed absolutely still, listening. At first, he heard only the mutter of distant talk. Then their bedroom door opened, and what he heard next so shocked him that he sat bolt upright.

"Don't worry, Mary. If Christmas gets lost this year, we'll survive. There are more important things than Christmas," his father said. "We'll do our best and that will have to do. Barney is old enough to understand"

"Isobel …" his mother began, but Dad broke in.

"She's too young to care. Your mother is the one who matters now."

One of them shut the door then. Barney strained his ears but he heard no more. After a couple of minutes, his eyes closed and, sliding back down under his covers, he slept.

In the morning, his father told him that his grandmother had had a stroke and Mom had caught an early flight to Toronto to look after her.

Why Grandma had to get sick just ten days before Christmas, Barney could not understand. She had always been healthy. She took lots of pills, but she did not even have a nap after lunch. His friend Jim's Nana was always "getting a little shut-eye," and Jim's Mom would shoo them outside so the old lady would not be disturbed. But Barney's grandma was not like that.

When he and Isobel were playing chase or monsters, or something a bit loud, Grandma had never ordered them out of the house, saying that "their racket was driving her mad." Once in a while, he had seen her quietly put on her coat and go out for what she called "a health walk." But she had told him more than once that she was tough as an old boot.

Barney had believed her.

When Isobel had run away from them once downtown, Grandma had dashed after her and caught her in no time, even though Isobel moved like lightning. Grandma had gone curling until last winter. She did not live with the Grants but she often visited. And, until now, he had never had to worry about her. She had seemed as strong and full of life as one of the two great chestnut trees in front of his house.

"What happened to Grandma, exactly?" he asked again at suppertime, knowing the answer, but hoping it might grow clearer or change.

"I've told you, Barney," his father groaned, "and it's Isobel's bedtime. Do me a favor and load the dishwasher, while I give her her bath."

Barney watched his little sister quit trying to lick the last trace of red Jell-O out of her bowl and begin banging it on the table.

"No baff! No baff!" she bellowed. Neither her brother nor her father paid any attention. She shouted "No bath" every night but, the minute she got into the tub, she was in heaven. Getting her out was the real challenge.

Barney watched Dad urging her up the stairs and sighed. Loading the dishwasher was not a job meant for a boy his age. His friends never did it. Unloading it, yes. Putting the cutlery away, certainly. But most parents insisted on lining the dishes up in a set way. Until tonight, his own parents had never asked him to take over this ticklish job.

I should do it all wrong, he thought. Then he won't ask me to do it tomorrow.

But he didn't. He had unloaded it lots of times, so he really did know what to do. While he put the spoons in, he thought about his grandma's stroke.

"Your grandmother is paralyzed down one side," his father had said. "She can't speak clearly, and she's in the hospital in Intensive Care."

He had gone on about Grandma's neighbor calling, and Mom managing to get a ticket on a plane leaving at five.

"She asked me to tell you she's sorry she couldn't wait to say goodbye, but she'll be back soon. And I was to give you her love," he finished.

Four days had gone by since then. Mom had phoned to say that, although Grandma's speech was still very garbled, it was clear from the way her face lit up that she recognized Mom. The doctor said it was important to have someone with her that she knew well.

"So I'm stuck here for a while, Barney, but I'm still hoping to come home soon," she had finished up.

"That's okay," Barney had told her, doing his best to sound grown-up. But it wasn't okay. It was awful. She had not said one word about Christmas.

Barney could not imagine Grandma unable to walk or talk, but he knew it was true because he could hear the panic in his mother's voice. So he didn't beg her to come home, even though he thought they needed her even more than Grandma did. Because Dad had been right. Their Christmas had been lost in the shuffle. And he, Barney, was the only one who seemed to notice.

He plunked the water glasses into the top tray in the dishwasher.

 DO NOT OPEN UNTIL CHRISTMAS

He could hear Isobel singing at the top of her lungs.

"Jingle Bells,

Batman smells,

Robin laid an egg.

The batmobile

Has lost its wheel

And joker played ballet."

It was her favorite song, and Barney could hear his father begging her to stop.

Isobel went right on yelling happily and splashing the water all over the floor. Barney, listening to her, grinned. Isobel's wickedness comforted him. It was so entirely normal. Maybe things would come out right yet.

He stacked the plates on their edges, waiting to hear her call, "Nigh-night, Bawnny!" When that moment came, she would expect him to be standing ready to catch thrown kisses and throw some back. Baby stuff. But she was only two. He could tell that she hadn't noticed that nobody was getting ready for Christmas at their house.

Barney looked around for dishes he might have missed. Isobel's Jell-O bowl and Dad's coffee cup seemed to be the last.

I'll ask Dad when he comes back down, he thought, adding the soap and slamming shut the door of the dishwasher. He still had the counter to wipe. He wouldn't have bothered any other time, but he wanted his father in a good mood. Then he might take time to talk things over, and Barney could remind him about all that still needed doing.

Dad came in, glanced at the kitchen, gave his son a tired grin, and picked up the newspaper. As he dropped into his big chair, Barney hurried to stand beside him.

"Dad …" he began. Then he hesitated. Should he start by asking about Grandma?

"What is it, Barnacle?"

Barnacle was a nickname from his baby days, when he had wanted them to carry him and had refused to let go when they tried to put him down. It was a good sign. They only used it now when they were especially fond of him. He took a deep breath and plunged in.

"Will Mom be home for Christmas?"

"I've already told you, she is going to try," his father said slowly. "You mustn't count on it, though. But if your grandmother is doing a bit better, and your Aunt Geraldine can get a flight from Halifax and arrange some time off, your mother hopes to get here. Maybe. But you mustn't be too disappointed if the plans fall through."

Barney stared at him. How could a boy his age not be disappointed if his mother was not able to share his Christmas? Isobel, too. She was always saying, "Me want Mommy, now!"

"I can't help it, son. It's tough for me, too," Dad said, putting down the paper and rubbing his eyes as though they hurt him.

"Christmas is only six days away now," Barney blurted, ignoring his father's words. "Everyone is getting ready. Nothing is ready here. All my friends have Christmas trees and their houses are decorated. At Jim's house, they have a Santa standing on the lawn and a reindeer on the roof. Its nose lights up like Rudolph's."

"I saw it," George Grant muttered. "It's obscene."

Barney ignored this. "But, Dad," he started in again.

His father took a deep breath. Barney could tell he was trying hard not to lose his temper.

"Taking care of you and Isobel is about all I can manage at the moment," he said. "I'll get us a tree tomorrow. It won't kill me to skip lunch this once. Apart from that, a big part of getting ready will have to be your job, son. Christmas is too much for me right now."

He laughed unsteadily, reached up and ruffled Barney's hair, and pushed the remote. A newscast came on, telling about some faraway earthquake. Barney ignored the solemn voice and the terrible pictures. He had his own disasters to deal with. He had to make Dad listen.

"But, Dad ..." he started in again, his voice rising.

"That's enough, Barnabas. Christmas or no Christmas, you need your sleep. Go to bed, spit-spot," Dad said. The words were ordinary enough but the voice was sharp.

"How about my story?" Barney mumbled, backing away a step.

"Read yourself a story for a change and get to bed. I couldn't stay awake long enough to read a bedtime story if my life depended on it," his father said.

Barney ran up the stairs, his eyes hot with tears. How could Dad be so mean? And how could he expect Barney to decorate the house and get everything ready? He couldn't, and that was all there was to it. His father hadn't said a word about kissing him goodnight.

Mom would never have sent him off like that.

Dad had not mentioned Barney's having a bath, but he'd left the water Isobel had used. Barney got in and added some hot. After he had played with Isobel's bath toys for a while, he felt calmer. He began thinking of things he might be able to do. He knew where they kept the Christmas decorations, in the big cupboard in the basement. Quite a few cards had come. He could stand them up on the mantel. If Dad brought a tree ...

Barney got out of the chilly bath water and dried himself sketchily. He put on his pajamas and looked for an easy book to read. He'd show Dad. At last, he found *Marvin's Best Christmas Present Ever.* He knew it practically by heart. He read it right through, hoping his father would come up after all and find him reading.

Marvin's father reminded him of his own, and he decided to creep down and see if Dad was in the mood for a hug.

George Grant sat slumped in the chair, sound asleep. Barney pushed the OFF button on the remote and kissed his father so softly he did not waken. Then, feeling a bit better, he crawled into bed.

When he came home from school the next day, Barney discovered a large box standing in the front hall. It was as big as Barney almost. *X-MAS TREE* it said on the side. *SPRUCE*. His father was not home. He must be fetching Isobel from nursery school. Well, Barney thought, he'd open it himself. He had trouble getting into the carton. The metal rods and bushy little plastic branches inside weren't at all like the fragrant dark evergreens they had bought every other year. It looked complicated. It did not smell one bit like a spruce tree.

"Dumb thing," Barney muttered. His dad would have to put it together. Barney had other jobs planned. He went back outside and set to work to make the best snowman in the history of the world. He intended it to look every bit as impressive as the reindeer on the neighbors' roof.

He had it over half done when the car pulled in. Dad got out and began undoing Isobel's car seat.

"Looks good, son," he called across to Barney. "Give me a hand with the groceries, will you?"

Barney was already at the back of the car, pulling out the bulging plastic bags. Determined to be helpful, he did hope his father was noticing.

"You are one neat kid," Dad said. "Did you see the tree? The man said it looks entirely lifelike, once it's put together. You can help me with it after supper."

Barney did his best to look pleased. He was glad when his small sister spoke up and saved him from having to lie about how well he liked the fake tree.

"Me hep you, Daddy. Me hep, too," Isobel announced, pounding her father's leg to get his full attention.

"Ouch!" Dad said. "Of course you can help, honey. You can hand us bits, maybe. After supper, that is."

Putting up that tree sounded easy. It wasn't. Also, there were the dishes and Isobel's bath, and stuff from school for his father to sign. By Barney's bedtime, the tree was standing upright and wearing lights, but that was all. It looked unfinished. Barney saw Dad's shoulders slump and heard him sigh as he stared at it. His thin hair stood on end and his disappointment was clear.

Christmas is getting lost, all right, Barney thought. This is what he meant. No time. No Mom.

Then he saw Isobel staring up at the undecorated tree, her eyes wide with wonder. He squared his shoulders. He would not let her Christmas be lost. He could fix it.

"Leave it to me, Dad," he found himself saying all at once, his dark eyes shining. "I can finish it all by myself."

He was sure he could. Almost sure, anyway.

He made a vow then and there. I, Barnabas Grant, vow to save my sister's Christmas.

"What a relief," Dad said, perking up a little. "I'll be waiting to see the excellent job. By the way, that snowman you're making

164   DO NOT OPEN UNTIL CHRISTMAS

looks promising."

Barney didn't want to spoil the surprise he was planning, so he did not answer. He had something else on his mind, too. He had an uneasy feeling that his father had forgotten a major event. It had been talked of the Sunday before, but then the telephone call had come from Grandma's neighbor, and everything else had been pushed aside. Barney had only remembered it himself that afternoon. He waited, but he knew he had to bring it up.

"Dad, are you remembering the Sunday school concert?" he asked, when his father finished telling him a very short story and was tucking him in.

"Oh, Lord," George Grant groaned. "When is it? I'd totally forgotten …"

"That's okay," Barney said. "You never come till it's almost over, anyway. No wonder you forgot. Isobel and I have to be there because we're performing. It's the day after tomorrow, Sunday, the 23rd."

"I'll probably be late again," his father said slowly. "I'll get Mrs. Holly to take you. And Isobel, too, of course. There's so much to do …"

He trailed off. Barney was glad he had mentioned it. He was sorry his father would not be there, but he never had been in the past. Mom came early, and Dad arrived in time to bring them home. The concert seemed far away. Barney was thinking about his snowman plan and how he would decorate the tree. Tomorrow would be Saturday. He'd have lots of time to get everything done.

Early the next morning, he waved as his dad drove off to do a long list of errands, taking Isobel to the babysitter's on the way. He had meant to take Barney there, too, but Barney had begged to be left on his own.

"Are you sure you'll be all right by yourself until we get back?" his father had asked again, as he zipped up Isobel's jacket. "Your mother would not approve of my leaving you, but you sound extremely busy."

"I am," Barney told him. "I've got stuff to do."

He waved goodbye to them and then ran to get started. He found the tree decorations just where he thought they would be. Behind them was another cardboard carton. Curious to see what had been hidden away in such a dark corner, he pried it open and peered inside. It was a Santa Claus costume! He had decided to do his best to rig his snowman out like Frosty, but Santa Claus would be even better. His dad would be amazed.

He began with the tree, but he hurried. At the end, he positively threw the tinsel on as messily as Isobel would have done. His Santa snowman was more exciting because it was all his own. He left the star for his father to do. It was too important for him to mess it up, somehow. Besides, he wanted to get out to finish the snowman.

It wasn't easy making that man of snow look like jolly old St. Nicholas. He ripped the hat a little pulling it onto the snowman's head. The suit was definitely not new, he noticed. There was a patch on one elbow. He left the pants in the box. Giving a snowman legs was beyond him.

The sun was setting when Dad and Isobel came home, but there was enough light to show his creation clearly. Barney stood tall. He could not remember ever feeling so proud. He waited for the grin he knew he would see on Dad's face.

His father stared at the marvelous snowman in wonder. He must be so stunned he could not think what to say. For a full two minutes, he just stared. Then he cleared his throat.

"Barney, that is stupendous, but I'm afraid, now I've seen it, I'll have to take it off him. The suit isn't really ours. But I'm glad you thought of it. It looks spectacular."

The bubble of excitement that had been growing bigger and bigger inside Barney broke. His snowman would be ruined. He made his face go stiff and fought to keep the tears from spilling down his cheeks.

But when they all got inside and beheld the tree, Isobel's cries of delight and Dad's astonished praise made up for the need to undress his Santa. After Dad carefully eased the suit off the snowman, Barney and Isobel found him a long scarf and cane, and his father actually arrived with an old top hat he had had since college days. The man of snow looked almost as fine as he had before. He was no longer Barney's dream but, maybe after a while, that would stop mattering.

On Saturday night, Dad not only took charge of Isobel's bath but Barney's, washing his hair and cutting his fingernails. Then it was Sunday afternoon and time to get ready for the concert. Barney drilled Isobel again on "Away in a Manger," which she was singing with the nursery class. His own Intermediate class was miming "A Visit from St. Nicholas" while he recited the words. He didn't have to practice. He'd known all the words since he was six. Mom had taught it to him, reciting it over and over herself, until he learned it without knowing he was doing so. She'd be proud if she could only be there to hear him. He thought his dad might want to hear him run through it, but he kept having to answer the phone.

"That's the most hopeful news we've had yet," Barney heard him say once. But he spoke in a hushed voice that told Barney that whatever the news was, it wasn't his business.

Mr. Holly came to pick them up at five. As they went out to the car, Barney heard his father say, "She's hoping for the best but, if things don't work out, Barney won't be too shocked. He's stopped asking. Isobel is only a baby, really, so it will be all right for her, whatever happens. The timing is so complicated, though. It will be a near thing."

"Just remember that we can take the children for Christmas," Mrs. Holly said. "No problem."

Barney's heart sank like a stone. He longed to run back to his bed and wrap himself up tight in his fat comforter, and stay there until his mother came to rescue him. Then he heard Dad say, "No, I can't discuss it, but I'm expecting glad tidings any second."

DO NOT OPEN UNTIL CHRISTMAS

Barney climbed into the waiting car. He rolled down his window.

"Come as soon as you can, Dad," he said shakily.

His father gave him a pretend punch on the jaw.

"I promise. See you later, son," he said.

"Yeah," croaked Barney. "See you, Dad."

Thank goodness Dad had said he didn't have to stick around with Isobel and "be responsible" at the concert. After the pot luck supper, he could leave her with the Hollys and go off with the other guys his age. He hated the other boys to see him with her trotting after him, especially when she was decked out in a flowery dress with ruffles and had little butterfly bows in her halo of bright curls.

✳

"Let us all join in 'Joy to the world,' number three on your carol sheet," Mrs. Mulligan, the Superintendent said.

As he stared at the page, Barney saw words he had never really noticed before.

Let every heart prepare him room

And heaven and nature sing ...

Sitting down next to Peter Mulligan, Barney thought of all he had done to "prepare him room." Well, to get ready for Christmas, anyway. The nativity figures were set up on the mantel, all but the baby Jesus, who was not put in the manger until Christmas Eve. He wasn't even sure his father had seen them yet. If he had, he had not said anything.

When he had realized Dad was not taking him shopping, he had come up with presents, too. He had wrapped up his black lamb for Isobel. He'd had it since he was born, but she was always asking to hold it. For his parents, he'd drawn pictures of the snowman dressed in a Santa suit. He had drawn them with great care, and he was sure they would love them.

"Look at my dopey sister," Peter hissed. "What a dork!"

Bonnie Mulligan, on her way to the stage with the nursery bunch, was waving wildly at her brother. He went red and turned his head away. Isobel danced straight up onto the stage and sang, with no mistakes her coach could detect. He waved at her.

When his class's turn came, Barney recited, tripping up once but getting all the reindeer names right and in order.

Then, after they had sung "Jingle Bells" a few times to bring him, Santa Claus, pack bulging, came stamping in, jingling like mad and calling out, "Ho, ho, ho!" Barney laughed and relaxed.

Two minutes later, disaster struck.

It was Isobel's moment to go forward and get her present from Santa and, at the sight of the towering personage waiting for her, she suddenly freaked out. She backed away, burst into tears, and looked around frantically.

"Bawny, Bawny, me want you wight now!" she sobbed.

For the second time that day, her big brother yearned to flee. Clenching his teeth and not looking to right or left, he got up and ran to her. When he leaned down to comfort her, she jumped at him, flung both arms around his neck, wrapped both legs around his waist, and clung on for dear life.

"Let go!" he growled, hugging her.

"No," Isobel howled.

"Hey, don't be so silly, Belly Button," he whispered into her ear. "Santa has a present for you. Go on."

"You come, too," she blubbered.

"Okay, okay," he said, hiding his flaming face against her.

Holding her tight in his arms, he lurched toward Santa Claus. The jolly red giant put a bag of candy and a little doll into the small girl's outstretched palm. The other hand was clutched tight around her brother's neck.

Then, to Barney's astonishment, Santa beckoned him to lean down. Isobel did not like it, but her brother bent closer.

"Well done, son," his father's voice murmured.

Barney gaped at him for one shocked second. Dad! His father was Santa! Then he forgot Santa Claus entirely.

"Mommy!" Isobel was screaming, beating her brother about the ears with ecstatic fists, "Mommy, Mommy, Mommy!"

Barney swung around and could not believe his eyes. His mother was standing right next to the steps leading down from the stage. Her smile outshone the brightest star. Barney would have flown like a bird to her if it had not been for his sister. He staggered halfway across the stage, with Isobel still holding fast to her hero, clinging on as tightly as a barnacle.

The audience began to laugh. Then a storm of applause broke out, and Peter Mulligan whistled through his teeth.

Barney, who had begged Dad not to saddle him with his sister, discovered that he did not mind how hard they laughed. He reached his mother and caught her and Isobel in one enormous hug. He didn't feel his sister's weight or blush at the growing rumpus made by the happy onlookers. Dad had been wrong when he said this Christmas would be lost. He, Barney, had gotten ready for it just as he had vowed he would. He had made up his mind not to let his parents steal Isobel's Christmas. And it had worked. He, with the help of Isobel herself and Mom and Dad, and everyone here, had kept it safe and sound and waiting for them.

Leaving his father stranded on the stage, giving out the rest of the gifts, Barney went to sit with his mother and sister. In less than an hour, the concert was over. Isobel, tired from so much excitement, stopped chattering and began to suck her thumb. Mother somehow got her into her coat, while Barney pulled on his jacket. Then, at the last moment, Dad appeared, as he had done every other year. But this time, he and his son exchanged knowing smiles.

As people left the hall, Mrs. Mulligan started playing "Silent Night" one last time. Some folks stopped to sing along, while others bundled up their children and pushed out into the starry darkness, calling back, "Merry Christmas!" A few of the congregation stopped to ask Mother how Grandma was.

"If you give me the keys, Isobel and I can wait in the van," Barney offered. He knew they wouldn't let him. They never did. They thought he was too young.

Mother smiled at him, and Dad slid the keys into his son's pocket. Isobel clutched his jacket sleeve.

"Come on, Bawny," she said sleepily.

Filled with astonished delight, Barnabas Grant turned to the door and started out on the homeward journey. Christmas had begun and it was going to be just fine.

What Made This Book Happen

Once, when I was talking to Rosemary Sutcliff about why we wrote what we did, she said, "We write the books that come to us, asking to be written." She was right. And it is true of short stories, too. The ones I've gathered together for this book all came to me as ideas wanting me to write them. When an idea like that arrives, I can hardly wait to begin.

I had written most of the stories over several years, when I got a book of stories from my friend Katherine Paterson last Christmas. As a friend read them aloud to me, I was reminded of my own Christmas stories. I realized that I probably had enough to fill such a book and wondered idly if I should collect them. A month or so later, I was at a church meeting and they were asking us to try to increase our donations, since the church had financial troubles. Suddenly, the story collection came to my mind, and I decided to see if I could raise some money by turning it into a book.

I enjoyed collecting them and listening to my computer read them aloud to me. They were almost all about boys. "A Present for Miss Potton" had been inspired by my nephew Brian, who had wanted to give his teacher a Christmas tree for a present. He was a little boy when he did this, and he is now a middle-aged man with four children of his own. But I liked the story.

A friend of mine told me about her little brother getting up while the rest of the family slept. He opened all his presents. He could not understand why his mother cried when she discovered what he had done. He, like Brian, is a man now with two daughters, but Will, in my story, is going to stay young and go on opening the parcels with his name on them.

I wrote "Without Beth" when Janet Lunn asked me to write a ghost story. After my mother's sister died, Mother saw her sitting in an audience at a church play. Mother's attention was called away and, when she turned back, my aunt had vanished, leaving an empty seat where she had been sitting.

"The Portable Christmas" came to me when a boy visiting at our house told me about having been dragged from one relation's house to another, never being allowed to play with his presents or have fun. I felt so sorry for him. I have told him how grateful I am to him for starting me off on this story, which is one of my favorites.

"The Boy Who Didn't Believe in Christmas" started off when my great nephew informed me that, even though he liked getting presents, he did not believe in Christmas—beginning with the story of Jesus being born.

I could go on, telling you what made me begin writing each story, but the incidents that start me writing are not the stories. Brian getting Miss Potton a tree will never become middle-aged. William is not my friend's grown-up brother. Eliza's sister Beth is not my aunt. Somehow, when the writer begins to shape the story, the characters that come onto the page take the place of the flesh-and-blood people who first gave them birth. It is mysterious and wonderful, and even the writer is surprised and delighted by the transformation.

Once in a while, it is not a person but an object that plants the seed. One of these started with a Santa Claus suit, another with a small ceramic Christmas tree I was given, a third with a walking doll I disliked. My great-grandfather took in a Barnardo boy like Scrap, and I was a counselor at Woodeden Camp one summer, and learned how to dance with a kid in a wheelchair.

Christmas isn't always an easy day for families. Sometimes it is lonely and sometimes it is disappointing. But in a story, you can find the joy in it, whether you are the writer of the story or the one who reads it. As you read these tales, may you have a Christmas that will make your heart sing.

Jean Little, 2014